"A date?" she said on a squeak of surprise.

"Yes. As I told you last night, we need to talk. About us." Jake reached for her hand and brought her fingers to his lips. "I want there to be an us, Marcie. Don't you?"

She smiled then, a wonderful smile that made him feel as if he could do anything if he put his mind to it. "Yes, I want there to be an us, too, but what about the rules?"

"For once in my life I'm going to ignore the rules." He brushed a curl back from her cheek.

"It could be dangerous," she said, her eyes sparkling.

"I'm willing to take the risk if you are. So what do you say?"

"You're the boss."

Dear Reader,

Welcome to the latest in our MARRYING THE BOSS miniseries. Over the following months, some of your favorite Harlequin Romance® authors will be bringing you a variety of tantalizing stories about love in the workplace!

Falling for the boss can mean trouble, so our gorgeous heroes and lively heroines all struggle to resist their feelings of attraction for each other. But somehow love always ends up top of the agenda. And it isn't just a nine-to-five affair.... Mixing business with pleasure carries on after hours—and ends in marriage!

Happy reading!

The Editors

Taming the Boss
Pamela Bauer &
Judy Kaye

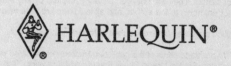

TORONTO • NEW YORK • LONDON
AMSTERDAM • PARIS • SYDNEY • HAMBURG
STOCKHOLM • ATHENS • TOKYO • MILAN • MADRID
PRAGUE • WARSAW • BUDAPEST • AUCKLAND

ISBN 0-373-03598-5

TAMING THE BOSS

First North American Publication 2000.

Copyright © 2000 by Pamela Bauer and Judy Kaye.

This edition published by arrangement with Harlequin Books S.A.

® and TM are trademarks of the publisher. Trademarks indicated with
® are registered in the United States Patent and Trademark Office, the
Canadian Trade Marks Office and in other countries.

Visit us at www.romance.net

Printed in U.S.A.

CHAPTER ONE

"I'VE found the perfect job for you."

Marcie MacLean took the chair across from the woman who had been not only her boss for the past five years, but her mentor, as well. "That's what I want to hear."

Sandra O'Neill, looking as sophisticated and poised today as she did every other day of the week, glanced up at Marcie over the rims of her designer reading glasses. "I have a client in a desperate situation."

"Are there any who *aren't* desperate?" Marcie quipped.

"It's the nature of the business and helps us be successful," Sandra reminded her.

And Marcie knew Temporarily Yours was definitely a success. Sandra had worked hard to earn the reputation the temp service had established for providing the most talented and efficient office professionals in the city. Marcie counted herself lucky to be one of her employees.

"I can't tell you how relieved I was to hear you say you wanted to work this week," Sandra told her. "I know you had hoped to take some time off to unpack your things, but this is a brand-new account and I want to send my best employee."

"Then it's a good thing I called." Marcie hadn't wanted to come in today. Having just moved into a new apartment, she and her sister were still living out of boxes. Yet as much as she would have liked the extra time to get settled in, there were bills to pay, including some hidden expenses she hadn't expected regarding the move. She couldn't afford to take a few days off...at least not now.

"Yes, it is." Sandra gave her a grateful smile. "There's another reason why I want you in this position. This is a new client and when he called I promised him he would find our service exceptional. Unfortunately, the first temp I sent him didn't work out, but I'm getting a second chance, which is why I need you to do your best."

"I'll do what I can," Marcie said with confidence. "But I can't imagine you sending out the wrong person on a job. You have an incredible talent for knowing just which person will work in which situation."

"And normally I have the luxury of making that decision, but with the business climate expanding, there's a real shortage of help, even in temps. You're the only one available who's qualified for this particular assignment. Actually, you're overqualified."

"Is it secretarial work?"

"Administrative." She flipped through a stack of cards until she found the one she wanted. "They're looking for someone to work closely with the CEO. Let's see here...." She perused the card, rattling off the duties involved. "Assist traders and analysts in maintaining legal documents, prepare and distribute finance reports, provide administrative support." She glanced up at Marcie. "Nothing you can't handle."

Marcie didn't contradict her.

"The good news is it's at the top of the pay scale. And if you stay the course, you get an additional bonus. Apparently, they've already gone through five temps."

"Five?"

Sandra nodded. "Fortunately, only one from this agency. So you see it's very important that you show them that this agency is not like most others." She tapped the edge of the card on the desk. "I must warn you, this is a tough assignment. The chief executive officer you're going to be working with has a reputation for being a hard taskmaster."

Marcie chuckled. "I figured there had to be a reason for five temps in five days. For the right money, I can put up with even the crabbiest of men as long as it's short term. And you know I'm not afraid of hard work."

"You don't need to tell me," Sandra said with a knowing smile. "It's why you're in such demand." She glanced at her watch. "They want you as soon as possible, so I've called for a taxi." Before Marcie could protest, she held up her hands. "Don't worry about the expense. The client's covering it."

Marcie was relieved. Normally, she took the bus to her assignments because she couldn't afford the luxury of a taxi.

Sandra handed her a time card. "Here's the client's name and address. The man you report to is Jake Campbell."

"Jake Campbell?" Marcie repeated, her breath catching in her throat.

Sandra glanced at the card. "Yes. He's the CEO of the firm." Seeing the startled look on Marcie's face, she asked, "You're not worried about what I said about his being difficult, are you?"

"No," she quickly denied. Her heart missed more than a couple of beats. It couldn't be the Jake Campbell she knew. It had to be a coincidence. Campbell was a common name and that particular Jake Campbell worked for another firm, not the one on her time card. But what Sandra had said about his being difficult did raise Marcie's suspicions. The Jake Campbell she knew had been one very difficult man.

"Taxi's here," the agency's receptionist said as she poked her head into Sandra's office.

"Do you know this Jake Campbell?" Marcie asked Sandra as she pulled on her coat.

"Not personally, but I've spoken to him on the phone. Don't worry, Marcie, in all the years you've worked for me I've never heard anything but praise for your work." She gave her a reassuring smile. "You can swim with the big fish."

Marcie wasn't so sure. It depended on what kind of fish were in the pond. At one time in her life she had nearly been gobbled up by a shark of a boss. The memory of that humiliation could still make her shudder...especially when he had the same name as the man on her time card.

As she rode in the taxi to her assignment, she told herself the man she was reporting to today couldn't be the one she had worked for. That firm had been small. This was one of the largest investment companies in the country. Certainly a man so ill-mannered wouldn't now be the CEO of such a prestigious firm.

Still, as she headed toward her assignment, she said a small prayer that she didn't know her temporary employer. Because if she did, the job was going to be even more difficult than Sandra had predicted. The last man she was going to assist in any financial matters was the man who had fired her five years ago.

Jake Campbell searched his entire desk for his plane ticket to the tax-investment seminar in Chicago. It wasn't there. He raked his hands through his hair in frustration.

He buzzed the outer office. "Could you come in here?"

Dead air reminded him that he was without an assistant. Steady, reliable Brenda had behaved impulsively for once in her life. She was sipping piña coladas on a sandy beach at a resort she called her honeymoon paradise. Her pleasure was his pain.

He raked a hand across his head and picked up the phone. He punched in the number for Temporarily Yours.

"It's Jake Campbell. I still don't have my temp. You said you were sending a *reliable* one this time."

"She's on the way," Sandra O'Neill said in a calming tone.

"Is she getting here in this century?" he snarled.

The woman at the other end sighed. "I know it's difficult being shorthanded, but if you would not growl—"

"I don't growl. And I have every right to expect that someone I'm paying good wages will behave in a competent manner," he said, trying not to sound as grouchy as he felt.

"Of course, which is why the person I'm sending today is the cream of the crop."

"If she's not, I just may have to fly to the Bahamas and drag my regular assistant back—even if she is on her honeymoon," he quipped.

The woman chuckled in his ear. "Do I need to warn this poor woman her boss is threatening to put a quick end to her honeymoon?"

"I don't think she gave anyone the number of where she's staying."

"Not if she's smart, she didn't."

Jake leaned back in his chair and sighed. "I can't believe she's gone. She's always been so dedicated. For her to just up and run away like that...well, it's certainly not like her."

Again Sandra chuckled. "That's the power of love. Makes people behave out of character. Once the honeymoon's over, she'll be back."

"She better be. I'm not sure I'll be able to retain my sanity if I have to put up with a temp for much longer."

"Trust me. You're going to like this one," Sandra said confidently. "She has excellent references."

He made a dubious sound. "I'm only taking a chance on her because you told me your agency is the best agency in town."

"It is. You'll see."

Jake ended the phone call and glanced at the pile of unanswered mail on his desk. He scooped it up in his arms and carried it to the outer office, dumping it in the middle of Brenda's desk.

Then he got himself a cup of coffee. He took one sip and grimaced. Was there a temp out there who could even make a decent cup of coffee, let alone efficiently handle the responsibilities of assistant to the CEO?

He sure hoped so. He didn't have time to fly to the Bahamas.

"Finance is on the second floor," the gray-haired security guard told Marcie as she checked in at the front desk of the investment firm. "You'll see the reception desk when you get off the elevator."

"Thanks." She signed the visitors' log and pinned the temporary badge to her lapel. Then she took the elevator to the second floor, which was a beehive of activity with employees scurrying about. They all wore tense expressions that matched Marcie's mood. "Guess I'm in the right place," she muttered under her breath. She walked up to the reception desk where a young woman sat, her fingers punching buttons on the phone as she repeatedly said, "Can you hold, please?" Seeing Marcie, she held up a finger, indicating she'd be with her momentarily. Finally, with a glance at Marcie's badge, she looked at her and said, "All the way to the back."

Marcie stepped around the office divider and saw a woman at a desk wearing a bright red suit and looking every bit as polished as her long, lacquered fingernails. Leaning over her was a bald man with a pencil behind one ear. Noticing Marcie, he straightened, offering her his hand.

"Fred Hanson. And this is Alicia Crosby." He introduced the woman beside him.

"Marcie MacLean. I'm from Temporarily Yours," she said as the two exchanged a furtive glance.

"Welcome," the red-suited woman said with a sympathetic smile. "You're in the right place. This is the finance department."

"Good." Marcie returned her smile. A quick glance across the room told her there were no vacant desks. "If you'd show me where to hang my coat and point me to my desk, I'll get started."

"Oh, you won't be out here," Alicia told her. "Your office is in EQ."

"EQ?" Marcie raised one eyebrow.

"Executive quarters." Alicia pointed a perfectly manicured red nail toward a section of the office separated by glass doors.

"Oh. Okay." Marcie tried to sound cheerful, but the closer she got to meeting Jake Campbell, the more uneasy she became.

It didn't help that Fred Hanson said, "Things are a little hectic around here today. I don't know if anyone told you, but the reason we need a temp is because Jake's assistant ran off and got married."

"Yes, and she didn't give any hint that she was going to be gone," Alicia added. "She just up and left."

"So her boss isn't exactly in a good mood, right?" Marcie concluded.

"You got it," Fred said with an apologetic grin. "If he bites your head off, try not to take it personally."

"Fred! You're going to frighten the poor woman," Alicia said with a click of her tongue. She tried to reassure Marcie. "It's true he's not happy with the disruption, but basically he's a decent guy. As long as you're capable and efficient, everything will be fine."

Marcie thought Fred looked as if he wanted to contradict that statement but decided against it.

"I appreciate the words of warning," Marcie told both of them. "Now, since I'm already late, maybe someone could introduce me to him?"

Neither one looked eager to take her to the CEO's office. Finally, Alicia said, "Sure. I'll do it."

Marcie followed her through a maze of desks and computers to what Alicia referred to as the inner sanctum. Once inside the glass doors she was shown to a plush office. Bright sunlight streamed through tall plate-glass windows that provided a beautiful view of the park across the street. There was every convenience she could imagine, including a small kitchenette.

While Alicia took Marcie's coat and hung it in the wardrobe, Marcie walked over to the desk and sat down. There were piles of unopened mail, memos and packages stacked high.

"She's been gone a week already," Alicia told her as Marcie moved a stack of mail aside to see the calendar. "Jake thought she would be back by now, but..." She trailed off with a shrug of her shoulders. "Come. I'll introduce you to your temporary boss." Alicia knocked on the impressive wood door, but there was no answer. "Guess he's not here. Why don't you become acquainted with everything and I'll go see if I can find him."

Marcie nodded and watched the woman leave. She walked over to the kitchenette, slipped her lunch inside the small refrigerator, then brewed a fresh pot of coffee. Feeling the start of a headache throbbing at her temples, she pulled a bottle of pain reliever from her purse. As she went to pop open the cap, it fell to the floor and rolled under the refrigerator.

Marcie got down on her hands and knees to try to retrieve the cap. It was while she was in such a position that she heard the office door open. She saw a pair of polished leather shoes, perfectly creased pants, a jacket covering a starched white shirt and tie.

Then she saw the man's face and had to stifle the gasp. His eyes were narrowed, his attention on a report in his hand as he strode across the room, but there was no mistaking his identity.

Marcie's worst fear had materialized. It was Jake Campbell. *The* Jake Campbell. The one who had been responsible for her failing her college course. The one who had treated her as if she were an idiot instead of an intern. The one who had fired her five years ago.

She wanted to slide right under that refrigerator. Disappear before he ever saw her kneeling there. But it was too late. As he passed the kitchenette, he saw her on the floor.

"Lose something?" he asked, his brows knitted together.

Slowly, she got to her feet, dusted off her hands on her skirt and faced him. "I got here a few minutes ago. I was taking some aspirin when the cap to my bottle..." she began but stopped when she saw the look on his face. It was a combination of wariness and impatience.

"Do I know you?" His tone was full of accusation.

"As a matter of fact, we have met before. I'm Marcie MacLean," she answered, offering him her hand.

"Marcie MacLean?" He stared at her as if she were a bug under a microscope.

"I was an intern at Davis and Meyers. You were one of the financial planners..." She trailed off, wishing he didn't look as if the memory were giving him a bad case of heartburn.

Suddenly, any confusion on his face vanished. In its place was a commanding authority. "What are you doing in my assistant's office?"

It would have been easy to cower beneath that piercing look, but she lifted her chin, determined not to be intimidated by him. "I'm your new temp. I understand you need an administrative assistant."

"Sandra O'Neill sent you?" he asked, his voice as incredulous as his face.

"Yes." Marcie's heart sank as she stared at the handsome, black-haired man towering over her. At six foot three, he dwarfed her five-foot-five frame. She tried not to shrink back from the penetrating green eyes, but it was difficult to stand tall when he was looking her up and down as if she were a new but defective piece of furniture.

She struggled to maintain her composure. "She said you were in desperate need of temporary help...so maybe you should tell me where I begin?"

He continued to stare. "There's been a mistake. I asked for Sandra's top administrative assistant with a financial background."

She smiled weakly. "That would be me."

"You?" A nasty chuckle rumbled from his throat. "If you're the best Sandra has to offer, then her business is in big trouble."

"I beg your pardon?" Marcie took a deep breath to try to stem the anger his comment aroused. "If you look at my references, they speak for themselves."

"I don't need to see your references. Or have you forgotten? I have firsthand experience of your incompetence."

The words stung. It was true she had made some mistakes as an intern in his office, but she was *not* incompetent. Yes, she had been young and a bit foolish, but she had also juggled many hats. Besides going to school and working as an intern, she had had to work two part-time jobs, as well, to support her younger sister.

"I've had a great deal more training and experience since I worked for you," she said calmly, then recited some of her references.

He fixed her with a penetrating gaze and said, "You can't honestly expect me to hire you after what happened the last time you worked for me. You are *not* the person for this job, Ms. MacLean. Don't bother making yourself at home. You're not staying." He started to walk toward his office.

"But you need help," she said, following him.

"Not yours." And with those words he stalked into his office, slamming the door behind him.

For a moment, Marcie stood motionless. She was getting the ax before she even had a chance to prove to him just how capable she was. Not that she wanted to work for such an impossible man. Memories of how he had reprimanded her in front of the entire office staff flashed in her mind.

He had been merciless. At the time, Marcie had thought that no intern could have stood up to such a scrutiny. He hadn't liked her from that very first day when she had walked into his office to tell him she had jammed the copy machine. He'd looked for reasons to criticize her, finding fault with nearly everything she did.

Working for Jake had been Marcie's worst nightmare, ending on the day she was called into the personnel office and given a written assessment of her performance as an intern. *Cannot recommend approval for completion of internship. Position terminated.*

Crushed by the scathing comments he had written, Marcie had been too humiliated to confront the man. Not that it would have done any good.

She glanced at the closed office door. The temptation to leave this very minute and not have another thing to do with Jake Campbell was great. In no time at all she could have her coat on, march right out the door and never look back.

Something stopped her. She couldn't let Sandra down for one. When nobody else had believed in her, Sandra O'Neill had been there for her. Nor could she afford to pass up a job that paid as well as this one. And she definitely needed the money.

But it was more than money and Sandra's faith in her that had her knocking on Jake Campbell's door. It was her determination to prove to him that she was not the irresponsible employee he thought she was.

Five years ago he had fired her for misusing the company's e-mail system. Believing there was no point in denying the unjust charge, she had remained quiet, accepting the blame for something she hadn't done.

Well, she was no longer young and inexperienced. The temptation to march into Jake's office and declare her innocence was great, yet she knew he wouldn't believe her today any more than he would have five years ago. Because she had no proof.

After all this time she didn't think she'd care what this man's opinion of her was, but she did. It was important to her that she show him that he had been wrong about her.

Determined to do just that, she knocked first, then opened his door. "Mr. Campbell, I need to speak to you." He looked surprised to see her walk in but, to her relief, didn't order her out.

He had removed his jacket and was now sitting behind an enormous mahogany desk. From the way the white cotton clung to his shoulders, she guessed he still worked out religiously at the health club. If anything, he was even broader than she remembered. She didn't need the distraction his chest provided and forced herself to look him in the eye when she spoke.

"I know I made some mistakes when I worked for you five years ago and I'm sorry. But that was a long time ago. I was young and inexperienced. If you would just look at my résumé, you'd see that I have the knowledge and the experience to do the job you require."

"That may be, but I'm afraid I can't take that chance," he said stiffly. "As much as I respect Sandra O'Neill's ability to hire competent help, I can't forget your past performance on the job. They weren't just mistakes. You disregarded an important company policy. As the saying goes, you can't make a silk purse out of a...well, let's just say I don't think it will work out."

Marcie swallowed back the anger that tempted to clog her throat. "I can do this job, Mr. Campbell, and if you have any doubts, all you have to do is check any of my references. Certainly five years of respectable work entitles me to a second chance?"

"That may be, but I'm going to call Sandra and ask for another temp." He reached for the phone.

"Go ahead, but she'll tell you there are none available."

He paused in his dialing. "What do you mean there are no other temps? That's what Temporarily Yours is—a temp service."

"Yes, but there's a shortage of help. For the time being, every single qualified employee is on assignment. So you see, it's me or no one." She tried not to sound smug, but she knew she failed.

"There are other agencies," he muttered.

"I hear you've nearly exhausted the list," she said cheekily, unable to resist reminding him that he had already tried five different temps. "Besides, no other agency has the reputation of Temporarily Yours. And by the time you place your request and they find someone, the day will be gone. I'm here, I'm qualified and I'm ready to work."

She expected him to say he'd rather go with no one, but she remembered he wasn't an impulsive man. She could see him mentally debating his options and knew he was softening toward her when he asked, "Do you know how to use our computer system?"

"Yes, of course," she said confidently. "And I know which end of the telephone to speak into," she added. "Look. If you don't give me a chance, you'll be in worse shape. I've seen the piles of mail on Brenda's desk and I can imagine what it's been like for you not to have an assistant for a week."

She pleaded her case, refusing to give in without a fight. The humiliation of dragging herself back to Sandra's office within an hour of being sent to work was more than Marcie was willing to bear. Besides, she *was* the best temp Sandra had in her company. She wanted the chance to show Jake Campbell that she had earned that spot at the top of the list. And that she was a trustworthy, reliable person.

As he contemplated her offer, a scowl marred his handsome face.

"So it's up to you. If you want Brenda's desk to stay the way it is, dismiss me. If you want to get down to business—*your* business—then keep me." It was a challenge, one she thought he might have rejected had not the phone lines lit up simultaneously. Calmly, Marcie reached across the mahogany desk and punched a button. "Jake Campbell's office. Could you hold?" She did the same thing with the second and third lines, as well.

He threw up his arms in surrender. "What choice do I have? I'm stuck. All right. Take the job. But only until Friday. That's what you get. One week."

"A week? But Sandra said the assignment would last until the end of the month!" She thought about the bonus she would receive if she stayed the entire time.

"That may be, but you have a week. If anything goes wrong in that time, you are done. Out. Finis. And I won't hesitate to turn in a bad work report on you to Sandra."

"You don't need to tell me that," she said soberly. "I have firsthand experience on that subject."

If she had hoped to make him feel a bit guilty, it didn't work. The man apparently had no conscience.

"Who's on the phone?" he demanded to know.

She told him which line had which caller, then scooted back out to her desk, glad to be away from those penetrating eyes. He had looked at her as if she were totally inept and that annoyed her almost as much as the tingle of pleasure she felt staring at those muscles bulging beneath his shirt.

She quickly pushed those thoughts aside. Maybe Jake Campbell felt stuck with her now, but she'd change his opinion of her. She hadn't gotten the nickname Marcie the Marvel for nothing.

Jake buzzed the outer office. "Could you come in here?"

Within seconds, Marcie was at his desk. "Yes, sir?"

He hated it when anyone called him sir, yet he was reluctant to allow her the privilege of familiarity. "We need to go over a few things," he said gruffly. She pulled up a chair beside him and listened as he explained her assignments. When he had finished, he said, "Got that?"

"Yes. Contracts go to legal, everything else to Alicia out front who'll make sure it gets routed through the appropriate channels." Marcie exchanged one stack of files for another, saying, "I found these on Brenda's desk. I believe they need your immediate attention."

Jake stared at the woman attempting to put his office back in order. He could hardly believe she was the same person who had single-handedly caused so much havoc at the investment firm.

She had definitely changed. And not just in her work habits. Wearing a gray suit with a white blouse, she looked nothing like the college student who had worn long flowered skirts and clingy knit tops that had bothered him just as much as her incompetent behavior. He noticed the curls that refused to be tamed into her chignon and wondered if she were to let her hair down whether it would bounce on her shoulders in springlike curls. The faint scent of a floral fragrance teased his nose, making him question if it was her shampoo or a perfume. Whatever it was, it was delightful and made him acutely aware of her presence.

"If there's nothing else, I'll go back to my desk," she said.

"No, that's it for now," he told her, then watched her walk away. Five years ago, she had been a shy teenager who was so nervous she had created more trouble simply by trying to stay out of his way. Now there was no lack of confidence in the way she walked. Nor did she shy away from him every time he spoke to her.

He felt a twinge of regret at having fired her. Yet at the time he'd really had no option. Trying to make a reputation for himself, he couldn't afford to lose clients because of someone else's errors. He had hoped that by hiring an intern he might have been able to train a future employee. What he hadn't expected was that he'd be assigned one who abused her Internet privileges.

She was the first person he had ever had to fire. And

the fact that she was a student had made it all the more difficult. He could still see that hurt look on her face when she returned from personnel after getting the news that he couldn't recommend her for completion of the course. For weeks after he let her go, he'd felt a twinge of remorse every time he saw a blond woman with curly hair.

Now she was back in his life. Sitting right outside his office. Organizing his files. Answering his phones. Distracting him with her blond hair and blue eyes, those shapely legs. He wished he didn't feel as if he'd just hired trouble.

CHAPTER TWO

JAKE punched his intercom button. "I need my mail, Ms. MacLean—before this millennium is over—if you please."

An unruffled voice drifted back to him. "All done, sir. Everything is in baskets on the cart outside your door. I didn't want to disturb you as long as you were on the phone."

"I'm not on the phone now."

"I presume you don't look at your 'junk' mail, but I've left it there for you to sort. Of course, I'd be happy to do it. Also, you can tell me if you want me to open anything marked Personal."

Jake's sigh was more of a growl in the back of his throat. "Bring everything in so we can go over it together."

"Yes, sir."

He had barely released the intercom button when she rapped on his door.

"What is she? Part rabbit?" he grumbled. Even Brenda couldn't jump that fast and she definitely would have won a gold medal in the office Olympics. "You don't need to knock when I've already given you permission to come in."

Marcie glided into the room with the cart in front of her. Without preamble, she handed him a sheaf of papers. "I've already drafted responses. If they meet with your approval, I'll get them into the mail right away."

"You answered my mail?"

"Isn't that what I'm supposed to do?" she asked with a perkiness he found annoying. "They're simply rough drafts. Of course, you'll need to pencil in any changes. I think if you look at them, you'll understand."

She was treating him as if he were the dim-witted one! He frowned, irritated by her presumptuous attitude, but one glance at the letters told him she had done an excellent job with the correspondence.

Amazingly, her responses sounded as if they'd been dictated by him. He looked up at her suspiciously. "How did you learn to do that?"

"Do what, sir?" Marcie stood at attention like a good little soldier, a gesture Jake found both off-putting and gratifying. He liked people to show respect and deference to him, but Marcie had refined it to a disconcerting art.

"Make these letters sound exactly like me."

"I have a good ear, sir." She paused for emphasis. "And we have met before."

"It takes more than an 'ear', and I hardly think either of us was at our best back then." He amazed himself with the admission. Marcie had been the problem all along, not him.

"Yes, sir. If you say so." Her lovely face was expressionless and the only animation came from a wayward curl that wound playfully in front of her ear.

"And stop calling me sir," he ordered.

Marcie looked him square in the eye and said, "Yes, sir."

She stood there so coolly, as if ice wouldn't melt in her mouth. And those legs! He'd nearly forgotten how attractive they were until she walked into his office that morning. Five years ago she'd been a leggy, untamed and glossy-haired filly in dire need of taming. Now she was a poised, supremely trained creature who could hide that mane of blond hair, but not those legs.

He was glad she couldn't read minds or she might have slapped him across the face for what he was thinking. He needed to remember that she was the woman he'd fired for unprofessional conduct.

It was a sobering thought that hit Jake like a splash of cold water. Just because the outer package was attractive didn't mean she was fit to run his office. He mustn't forget that although she appeared to be proficient, she was still the young woman who had broken rules and created chaos.

"I'm going to need you to arrange a conference call for these people." He handed her a list with several names on it. "I've indicated the times that are convenient. Set it up and get back to me by four," he snapped. "And see what kind of a mess has been made of the filing systems in Brenda's absence."

Marcie backed toward the door. In her haste, she nearly knocked a sculptured head of Beethoven off a carved teakwood stand. Hugging the tottering head close to her bosom and clutching the raft of papers to her belly, she backed out of the room.

It wasn't long before she slunk back in to replace the head. For just one moment the composure and sophistication slipped. Jake wanted to glare at her, but it took all he had just to hide his smile.

Marcie saw the ghost of a smile before she closed the door behind her. Drat the man! He was actually enjoying her discomfiture! Jake Campbell was playing with her the way a cat toys with a mouse—until he tires of the game and kills it.

"Sandra O'Neill, what have you gotten me into?" she moaned. The day was barely half over and she was already exhausted. Brenda would be lucky if she wasn't sleeping through her honeymoon. Hoping the newly-weds would have a spat of major proportions that would bring Brenda home sooner than expected, Marcie went to work at her desk.

By the time she'd finished the last of the correspondence, she discovered to her dismay that it was almost seven o'clock. In her effort to give Jake Campbell no reason to criticize her performance, she'd completely lost track of time. She was just shutting down her computer when he came out of his office.

"You're still here?" he asked bluntly, surprised by her presence.

He'd freshened up in his executive washroom, changed his shirt and tie and was obviously on his way out for dinner. She caught a subtle whiff of cologne and wondered if his evening plans included a woman.

"The letters are done and will go out tomorrow. Unless, that is, you'd like me to take them to the airport post office so they can still go out tonight. It's open twenty-four hours."

"That won't be necessary," he told her, his eyes narrowing.

"I have some ideas for the filing. It seems that Brenda has a very...unique...method of filing and no one else seems able to understand it. I think I can work a compromise—"

"Do whatever it takes. Just get it done," he interrupted her, apparently impatient to be gone. "Are you ready to leave?"

"Yes," Marcie said, a note of weariness creeping into her voice. She could see by the way he waited at

the outer glass doors he expected her to walk out with
him. He probably didn't trust her to lock the place up.

She grabbed her coat, watched him lock up the office, then walked with him to the elevator. To her surprise, people still sat at their desks working. Since Jake
didn't look surprised, she could only assume it wasn't
uncommon for his employees to work late into the evening.

At the elevator he held the door for her, then pressed
the button that would take them to the underground
garage. She reached over and punched the number for
the ground floor.

"You didn't drive to work?" he asked.

She shook her head. In the close confines of the elevator, she was acutely aware of his presence. She was
grateful the ride was a short one because being shut up
with him in a tiny compartment did funny things to her
stomach.

"Brenda has a spot in the garage you're welcome to
use," he told her.

"Thank you, but that won't be necessary," she said
as the doors slid open onto the main floor. She stepped
out quickly, saying, "Have a nice evening."

She hurried across the lobby, relieved that she hadn't
had to admit that she didn't own a car. She started
walking toward the bus stop. As she waited on the
corner for the light to change, she saw a shiny black
Porsche exit the garage. Jake was seated behind the
wheel. Curiosity had her wondering where he was going and with whom.

When the walk light appeared, she forced her attention back to the crowded intersection. Jake Campbell's
social life was of no concern to her and she'd be wise

to remember that. There was only one thing she needed to worry about—impressing him with her office skills.

And she had done that today. She recalled the look of admiration in his eyes when he'd seen the order she'd restored to Brenda's workstation. He had quizzed her ruthlessly as to where she placed everything, but he had been unable to find fault with a single thing.

It hadn't been an easy task, and by the time she reached the bus stop, she was grateful to see an open space on the bench. She dropped onto it in sheer exhaustion. When the big, diesel-spewing city bus pulled up, she was relieved to see that plenty of seats were available.

The ride home had never seemed longer. It was on weary legs that she climbed the steps to her apartment. She was hungry, tired and wanted nothing more than to soak in a hot bath and go to bed. Yet she knew her day wasn't over simply because she had left work.

"You look tired," her sister Peggy greeted her as soon as she opened the door.

"I've had a long day. A really long day." She hung up her coat, kicked off her shoes and dragged her weary body over to the sparsely furnished living room where she plopped down onto the sofa. "It was my first day on a job and things were hectic," Marcie said, rubbing her temples with her fingertips.

"This was supposed to be your week off."

"I know, but the money's too good to pass up." She looked at her sister then and saw that she was pulling on her jacket. "You going somewhere?"

"Study group for chemistry," she answered, tugging on her zipper.

Marcie saw her sister's backpack beside the door. One of the reasons they had chosen this apartment was so that Peggy could be closer to the university where she was enrolled as a student.

"And you wanted me to sit with Emma." Marcie groaned. "Oh, Peg, I'm sorry. I should have come home earlier, but I was working so hard I lost track of time."

"It's all right. You're here now," she said lightly.

"You're not going to be late, are you?"

"No, not that it matters. It's really more of a drop-in group. People come and go all evening."

"That's good. Is Emma already in bed?" Emma was Marcie's four-year-old niece. She and Peggy had lived with Marcie ever since the day she was born, which made Marcie feel more like a second mother to the child than an aunt.

"Mmm-hmm. I put her down right after dinner because she said she didn't feel well. I hope she's not getting the flu."

"Did she have a fever?"

"Only a slight one, but I gave her some children's pain reliever and that took care of it." She hoisted her backpack over her shoulder. "You will keep an eye on her, won't you? Fevers have a way of spiking at night."

"Don't worry. I'll take good care of her," Marcie told her, the way she had done so often in the past. She got up to walk over to the door so she could lock it after her sister left.

"I know you will." She pointed a finger at Marcie and said, "And take care of yourself, too. I worry about you when you work such long hours. I really wish you hadn't postponed your holiday. If we need extra money, I'm sure I could get more hours at the café."

Marcie gave her sister a hug, touched by her concern. "You do enough as it is. You concentrate on your studies and let me worry about the money, okay?"

"All right. I better go. If you're hungry, there's some leftover stew in the refrigerator."

Marcie was hungry, but she couldn't even think about eating until she had checked on her niece. As soon as Peggy had gone, she tiptoed into the bedroom where Emma lay asleep on the bed. The only light in the room came from a small porcelain angel whose face and wings gave off a warm glow.

Carefully, Marcie placed a hand on the four-year-old's forehead. It was slightly warm but not burning up with fever. She sat for a few moments on the side of the bed, looking at her niece, loving the picture of innocence she made. Tucked beneath one arm was a raggedy-looking bunny, the satin lining on its ears rubbed away by tiny fingers.

Marcie liked looking at Emma. She was such a beautiful child and had such a sunny disposition. When Peggy had become pregnant as a teen, Marcie had worried that the responsibility of motherhood would overwhelm both of them. Being a single parent was never easy, and for a teenager who hadn't even finished high school, it meant sacrifices a lot of teens didn't want to make. That's why Marcie had done everything she could to help her sister.

It had been a struggle and still was—especially with Peggy going to school, but helping to raise Emma was a joy that Marcie wouldn't have traded for anything. Any sacrifices she had made to keep the family together had been worth it.

She bent to place a butterfly kiss on her niece's forehead. Emma stirred but didn't wake.

"Get your sleep, little one, and you'll feel better

tomorrow,'' Marcie said softly, then tiptoed back out of the room.

In the kitchen she found the leftover stew, which she heated in the microwave. She was halfway through her meal when Emma appeared in the doorway.

"Can I have a drink of water?'' the small child croaked.

"Does your throat hurt?'' Marcie asked, getting up to get her a glass.

She nodded miserably. "And my ear.''

Marcie gave her the water and watched as she took a sip, then handed it back.

"Where's my mommy?''

"She had to go to school. Remember?''

"I wish she was home,'' the little girl said on the verge of tears.

Marcie scooped her up into her arms. "She'll be back in just a little bit. How about if I tuck you in and read you a story?''

Emma rested her head against Marcie's shoulder. "The mouse one?''

"Sure. The mouse one it is,'' Marcie said, carrying her back to her room.

Later, after Emma had fallen back asleep, Marcie was finally able to do what she had come home to do. Take a bath and climb into bed. By the time she pulled back the covers, Peggy still wasn't home. Marcie automatically reached for a novel to read while she waited for her sister to return.

It was a habit she had never broken—waiting up for her sister. Ever since their mother had died when Marcie was only nineteen, she had taken over the role of parent in Peggy's life. It hadn't been easy, especially when her sister had been a rebellious high school teen.

Now that Peggy was twenty-one, Marcie knew she didn't need her to be a parent, yet it was hard to let go of that responsibility.

That's why when Peggy strolled in later than expected, Marcie acted more like a mother than a sister.

"What are you doing up? I thought you'd be in bed," Peggy said when she saw that Marcie was in the kitchen.

"I was worried about you. It's late."

"I know, I'm sorry. I would have called, but I thought you'd be asleep." She hummed as she put away her things.

Suspicious of her sister's obvious good mood, Marcie asked, "Were you studying all this time?"

"Uh-uh. I stopped for coffee."

Marcie shoved her hands to her waist. "With the members of your study group?"

A sly smile spread across her sister's face. "Actually, it was with an old friend. Remember Tim Carlton?"

"The skinny kid with the stringy hair and glasses who used to live down the street from us?"

She nodded. "He wears contacts now and his hair is cut short—military-style."

"Everyone was always picking on him because he was so small," Marcie reflected wistfully.

"He's not anymore. You wouldn't even recognize him. I didn't. He's tall and he's in very good shape. He said it's from being in the navy. He spent four years in the service after high school. Do you know he's traveled all over the world?"

"How interesting," Marcie observed, not missing the sparkle in her sister's eye. "So how did you meet up with him again?"

"He came into the café one day and looked at me with this half grin on his face. I knew he looked familiar, but it wasn't until he started asking all sorts of questions about the old neighborhood that I realized who he was."

"He's changed that much?"

"Oh, yes." She sighed. "I never realized he had such blue eyes."

"That blue, eh?"

"Mmm-hmm," she said absently. "Isn't it a small world? I mean, who would have thought I'd run into an old friend while working at the café?"

From the dreamy look on her sister's face, Marcie knew that it was more than a reunion of old friends. "Is he in your chemistry class?"

"No, but he had to do some research on campus this evening, so we met for coffee afterward."

"Sounds like you had fun. You've been seeing him for a while, then?"

Peggy blushed and said, "For a while." As if suddenly aware that she was piquing her sister's curiosity, she changed the subject. "So how's Emma? Is she feverish?"

"She seems to be okay, although she did wake up and complain about her throat and her ear. I don't think she has a fever, though."

"That's good. She'll probably be fine tomorrow."

Only Emma wasn't well the following morning. Her tiny face was flushed, her forehead warm.

"I'm not going to be able to take her to day care," Peggy said to Marcie as they both stood in the bedroom doorway watching the little girl who had fallen back to sleep.

"You think she's running a temperature?"

Peggy nodded soberly, then led her sister into the living room. "Of all the days for her to be sick."

"You can't miss school today?"

"It's not my classes I'm worried about. I'm supposed to take a placement exam this morning. My boss was kind enough to juggle my schedule so I could get the time off and now it's all for nothing." Peggy flopped down onto the sofa, covered her face with her hands and moaned, "This can't be happening to me."

"I wish I could help, but I just started a new job yesterday. And this guy is a tyrant the way it is."

Peggy waved a hand. "No, I can't expect you to take time off." She pushed the hair back from her forehead. "The problem is the stupid exam is only offered twice a year. If I don't take it today, I can't take it until next fall, which means my courses will be out of sequence."

Marcie knew what a struggle it was to go to school, work a full-time job and raise a child. Peggy had worked hard to do all three and she was so close to finishing her university courses. She hated to see her fall behind because of something out of her control.

Before Marcie had left the office yesterday, she'd noticed that Jake Campbell was scheduled to be in a meeting that morning. Three hours had been blocked off on Brenda's calendar with the words, "Jake—meeting, off-site."

"I just remembered something," she told Peggy. "Maybe it's not a problem for me to take a couple of hours off. My boss is going to be in a meeting all morning."

Peggy looked at her hopefully. "I can't ask you to do that. You just said it's only your second day on the job."

"Yes, but I honestly don't think it'll be a problem. Besides, I want to do it."

"Are you sure?"

Marcie nodded. "Yes. I'll phone the office and let them know I'll be a little late. You go take your exam and I'll take care of Emma."

Peggy hesitated only a moment. "You're sure now that you won't get into any trouble?"

"It'll be fine. I told you. My boss is out of the office this morning. I'll stay late and make up for the lost time."

Peggy gave her sister a hug. "Thanks a bunch, sis."

Marcie had it all figured out. If she arrived at work by ten-thirty, she'd still get there before her boss. And if he made a fuss about the lost time, she'd stay late that evening. No matter what, Jake Campbell was going to have no cause to be upset with her.

"Oh-oh. Somebody's late," Alicia remarked in an aside she wanted Marcie to hear as she passed her desk later that morning.

"Hello" was all Marcie said, plastering a carefree smile on her face.

She knew many eyes were on her as she walked toward the executive quarters. Thanks, no doubt, to Alicia. She could just imagine the immaculately coiffed woman announcing to the entire office that the temp couldn't even make it to work on time her second day on the job.

"At least you're still here."

"Why wouldn't I be?" Marcie couldn't resist asking.

Alicia simply shrugged. "After what happened with

the previous temps, people in the office are taking bets as to how long you'll last.''

So much for the sincerity of her welcome yesterday, Marcie thought cynically. She knew it was Sandra O'Neill's protocol not to have any of her employees become involved in office politics. However, it was a little late to be worrying about that, considering she and Jake had a nasty little bit of history together already.

''I plan to stay until Brenda returns,'' she stated with false bravado.

''That's what the others said, too.'' Alicia gave her a smile that held a warning.

Marcie knew it was time to end the conversation. She excused herself and took refuge in her office. Maybe the woman had simply wanted to warn her of what she was up against, but Marcie needed no warnings. She knew exactly what it would be like to work for Jake Campbell.

As for the office bets, she didn't care what Alicia or any of the other employees in the office thought about her performance. She had come to do a job and she would do it. No matter what anyone said. No matter how difficult Jake Campbell wanted to be. This time, he would have no cause to dismiss her.

The very thought of her boss could cause her hair to prickle on her skin. That's why she was grateful he wasn't back from his off-site meeting when she entered her office. She slipped her lunch in the refrigerator, then went straight to work, not stopping until she heard the door open.

She glanced up to see Jake striding toward her, a scowl on his face.

''We're not on flex hours here, Ms. MacLean,'' he

said in an ominous tone that held more than a hint of a warning.

"It's true that I was late, but I can explain."

He held up a hand. "Save your explanations. I think there's something crucial that needs to be said. The rules of this office exist for a reason. You are expected to follow those rules if you want to remain employed here."

"I realize that and I didn't want to be late this morning, but something came up and it said on Brenda's calendar that you were going to be off-site this morning," she told him calmly, despite the panic that rose in her throat, threatening to give her voice a wobbly tone.

"Yes, off-site with my administrative assistant," he pointed out in a steely voice.

She swallowed with difficulty. "I was supposed to go with you?"

"Yes. That is your job. To *assist* me." He was leaning over her desk, pinning her with his angry green eyes.

"Then why didn't you mention this to me yesterday?"

"Because I didn't expect that on your second day of work you'd come in several hours late," he said in a nasty tone.

"I'm sorry. I didn't realize," she apologized. "I assumed from what Brenda had written that it meant you'd be out of the office this morning and it wouldn't matter if I took a few hours off. I phoned in to let the others know—"

Again he held up his hands and interrupted her. "Whom did you call? I received no message."

Puzzled, she said, "I don't understand. I did call and I had a good excuse for being late."

"Spare me the flimsy excuses. I've had a rough enough morning without listening to you try to justify leaving me in a bind."

"It's not a flimsy excuse," she said, annoyed that he would even suggest it was. "I had a family emergency."

It was then that he noticed the picture of Emma she had set on the desk. "I suppose you're going to tell me you had a sick child at home."

"Yes, as a matter of fact, I did."

"Maybe in the future you could get the child's father to sit with her when she's ill," he advised.

"I would be most willing to do just that—if she had a father."

He raked a hand across the back of his neck, looking as if he wanted to say more, but he simply said, "Bring the Henderson files and come into my office."

The last place she wanted to be was alone with him in his office. She already had one huge strike against her—her history. Now she had earned another one. He was probably just itching to find one more thing with which to trip her up so he could call Sandra and send her packing.

Marcie couldn't let him do it. From this moment on she would be an exemplary employee. Better than exemplary. And she was.

She listened intently, followed his every direction and performed every task he gave her. Not once did she stop or ask for a break. When her stomach growled, she could see by the look on his face that he had heard.

"It's after one," she pointed out.

"And you need your break."

"No, I need lunch. If you want me to order in something for you, we can keep on working," she suggested. "We've missed the lunch cart, but there's a deli right around the corner."

"That would help. Otherwise we're never going to get caught up."

"Then we'll have a working lunch. What can I get for you?" she asked as she reached for the phone.

His hand stopped hers in midair, the contact sending a tiny zap of pleasure through her. "I'll get it," he said, then picked up the phone. "I'm having pastrami on rye with hot pepper cheese. What about you?"

"Oh, you don't need to order anything for me. I brought my lunch. It's in the refrigerator."

"Do you like pastrami?"

"Well, yes, but it's not necessary."

He ignored her protest and dialed the deli. He ordered two pastrami sandwiches and two coleslaw. "It'll be here in about ten minutes," he told her as he hung up the phone.

Marcie nodded. "Thanks."

When she had suggested they have a working lunch, she thought they would continue to review documents while they ate. She didn't expect that he'd set aside the financial reports and actually devote time to eating. It was one thing to sit next to Jake Campbell and discuss business. Quite another to try to make small talk over a meal.

When the food arrived, he cleared a section at the end of the conference table, pushing aside the stacks of reports they had been working on. "There are beverages in the refrigerator, Marcie."

It was the first time he had called her Marcie since

she had been there. The way her name rolled off his lips made it sound as if they were good friends.

"What can I bring you?" she asked.

"Soda's fine."

"Glass?"

"No, I drink it straight from the can."

She nodded, then disappeared into the outer office, where she went directly to the refrigerator and pulled out two cans of soda. Then she took a deep breath, trying to still her rapidly beating heart before going back into his office.

"I can get plates and utensils if you think we need them," she said before sitting down across from him.

"Not necessary." He held up a plastic fork. "Might as well use these."

For the first time he didn't look so serious and Marcie discovered that when he wasn't talking business, he became much more relaxed. It gave her hope that beneath that steely exterior there actually beat a warm heart. When he relayed a humorous anecdote that he had heard at the off-site investment meeting that morning, she changed her initial opinion of him. Maybe he did have a sense of humor after all.

They had only been eating for a few minutes when he reached for his can of soda. He slipped his finger under the pull tab and a geyser burst into the air, spilling over his lunch, foaming onto his clothes.

"What the...?" he spluttered, all traces of friendliness disappearing. "Did you shake this?" He glared at her in an accusatory manner.

"Of course I didn't," she replied hotly, jumping to her feet to mop up the soda with her napkin. She could see that a sponge was what she needed and hurried out to find one while he disappeared into his private washroom.

When he came out again, she was seated at the table, all traces of the spill gone except for the soggy sandwich at his place. On his shirt was a large wet spot where he had obviously tried to wash away the spill. The scowl was back in place.

"I'm sorry, but even you must realize that it wasn't my fault," she said in her own defense as he sat back down at the table.

"What do you mean, *even me*?"

"You always think the worst of me. It's been that way since the very first day I began my internship." She tried to continue eating, but the sandwich tasted like sandpaper.

"Is it any wonder? This kind of stuff happens when you're in the room." He gestured to his wet shirt.

She was tempted to get up and walk right out the door. Leave him without *any* help, not even a temp. If she told Sandra what this man was like, she'd understand.

Or would she? After all, this was the professional world and Marcie was expected to be able to work in difficult situations. And she had earned such a respectable reputation precisely because she didn't let her emotions spill over into her work. If she left now, that reputation would be damaged. She stiffened her spine.

"Yes, I know, and copiers get stuck and computers get zapped. Of course, none of that happens to anybody else, so it must be me. I must have a defective part," she drawled sarcastically. When he didn't disagree, she slammed the remainder of her sandwich onto the table. "I'm done." She scooped up what was left of her lunch and stuffed it into the deli bag.

"Done? You can't leave. You agreed to stay until Friday," he reminded her.

"Leave?" She chuckled sardonically. "I said I was done with my lunch." She continued to cram papers and containers back into the bag. "I'm not going anywhere. You're stuck with me, remember?"

Relief briefly flashed in his eyes, then he said, "This wasn't a good idea—working through your lunch hour. You need to take a break." He glanced at his watch. "It's almost two. I'll expect you back by half past."

"All right." With as much dignity as she could muster, she walked out of the room. Once outside his office, she heaved a sigh of relief. She felt as if she had spent the past few hours in a duel of wits. The work had been challenging, but she had risen to the occasion. And if Jake Campbell were honest, he'd say she had done a good job, too.

But what she needed right now was some air. She grabbed her coat and headed for the elevators. A brisk walk would work wonders for her state of mind and was exactly what she needed to cool down from the heat that always managed to invade her body whenever he was around. It was only her second day and already she couldn't be in the same room without getting a little weak in the knees. How was she going to survive until the end of the assignment?

CHAPTER THREE

IT WASN'T long after Jake had sent Marcie on her break that Brenda phoned. Instead of telling him the news he wanted to hear—that she was on her way home—she told him she and her dearly beloved had won scads of money gambling and had decided to take an extended holiday. She hated leaving him in a pinch, but all those weeks of accumulated vacation time that she had never used because she had been such a dedicated employee—she was using now. She wouldn't be back until next month.

Jake stared at the receiver. Love had truly destroyed his assistant's brain cells. *Another month*? Whatever would he do?

Of course he knew there was only one thing he could do. He picked up the phone again and called Sandra O'Neill.

"Jake, I bet I know why you're calling," Sandra said when he identified himself. "You want to tell me how pleased you are with Marcie."

He suppressed the chuckle that wanted to escape. "Not exactly."

"Surely you don't have a complaint?"

"We're getting used to each other," he said evasively, then added, "The reason I'm calling is to let you know that I'm going to need a temp for an additional four weeks. I hope you can accommodate my request."

"Let me check." There was a brief pause, then he

heard her say, "Yes, I do believe I can juggle the schedule so that you can keep Marcie until the middle of next month."

"Doesn't she have other obligations already in place?"

"Marcie's always in demand, but there is no one who could work as well for you as she does. She's perfect for what you require."

"Perfect" was hardly the adjective he would have used. He glanced down at the spot on his shirt that was still damp. It was true that she was much more efficient than she had been as an intern, impressing him with her knowledge of the financial world, but could he trust her to run his office for the next month?

And there was his trip to Chicago. Brenda was supposed to accompany him to the tax seminar next week. She always went with him to conferences, acting as his right hand, keeping him organized. But instead of solid, steady Brenda who never missed a beat, he would have to take unpredictable, unreliable Marcie. How would he survive a business trip when she couldn't get through a regular working day without some minor catastrophe?

"Don't worry about a thing, Jake. Marcie is yours until the fifteenth of next month." And with a cheery goodbye, she rang off.

He was still pondering the situation when Marcie returned from her break.

"I'm back," she announced, sticking her lovely blond head into his office.

"Good. I want to talk to you."

Her cheeks were rosy, her hair less confined than when she'd left. Curly tendrils framed her face and once more he had the urge to see what that hair looked like without the clips and pins.

"Your cheeks are red." He didn't realize he had voiced his thoughts until he heard her respond.

"Oh, that's because I went outside. The sun is shining, but the wind is brisk," she told him, looking refreshed and healthy. "Typical March weather. Are we working on the Henderson project?"

"In a minute. I'd like to talk to you first." He gestured for her to take a chair.

As she sat, her skirt slid partway up her thigh, allowing him a glimpse of her shapely legs. "What is it you want to talk about?" she asked primly.

He forced his eyes back to her face. "I'm offering you a temporary position for another four weeks."

She looked completely taken aback. "I don't know what to say. Is this a compliment or are you that desperate?"

"Both," he answered. "Brenda's extending her vacation, which means I need someone to take her place until the middle of next month."

She stared at him suspiciously. "And you think I want the job?"

Was she playing a game with him? If she was, he could play that game, as well. "It comes with bonus pay." He leaned back in his chair, steepling his fingers at his lips.

He could see she was tempted to say yes, but she didn't. "I'll have to check with Sandra O'Neill before I give you an answer."

He spread his hands in midair. "No need. I've already spoken to her and she told me that she's comfortable with the offer."

"Then I guess I stay on," she said with a lift of eyebrow.

"Good. That settles that." He sat forward. "Swing your chair around to this side of my desk. If you're going to be working here for the next month, you need to know how to access certain files." He reached for his computer mouse.

"Brenda left instructions in her desk, so I've already familiarized myself with her PC, but I did have a few questions."

So she had already figured out how to access the files. *That* was certainly a change from five years ago. "One other thing you should know," he told her as she pushed her chair around the side of the desk. "I'm leaving for Chicago next Wednesday. Brenda was supposed to go with me, so I'll expect you to take her place."

"You mean fly in and fly out the same day, right?"

"No, I mean stay overnight in a hotel, probably two nights. We'll be there for a couple of days."

He could see by the look on her face that it wasn't what she wanted to hear. Some of her cool composure slipped.

"Is it going to be a problem—your being gone overnight?" he asked, wondering if she was worried about her child.

She hesitated only a moment before saying, "No, I can work it out."

"Good." He went on to explain how to access the files pertinent to the assignments she would be given, all the while acutely aware of her sitting next to him. All day long his nostrils had been teased by her flowery scent. It was so unlike the strong, bold perfumes that so many of his women friends wore. It was subtle and made his mind wander from the project at hand.

As she leaned her head closer to his, he had to remind himself that she was here to learn how to use the computer. There was no point in thinking of her in the same way as the women he dated, yet as hard as he tried, he couldn't prevent his curiosity from wondering just who Marcie MacLean really was. Was there a man in her life? She had said her daughter didn't have a father, but that didn't mean she didn't have a boyfriend. He had a hard time believing that a woman as lovely as she was would lack for companionship.

"I'm ready," she told him, interrupting his musings.

He realized that he had been staring at her. He forced his attention to the computer screen, determined not to think of her as anything but the office temp.

It didn't work. When her sleeve brushed his, he wanted to prolong the contact. And then there was her hair. As he gave her a tutorial on computer programs, there was one thought that kept nagging at his mind.

Would she let that hair down at the end of the day?

"Thank goodness it's Friday," Marcie said as she sank onto the sofa in her apartment.

"How many hours did you put in this week?" Peggy asked, taking the chair across from her.

"Too many." She suppressed a yawn. "The extra time will be nice on my paycheck, but I'm exhausted. Tomorrow I'm going to do absolutely nothing."

Peggy groaned. "Does that mean you don't want to go with me and Emma to the Children's Museum? Now that she's feeling better, I'd like to treat her to something special."

"It sounds like fun, but do we have enough money

in the goodie jar for that?'' Marcie and Peggy had an old pickle jar they kept in the cupboard where they deposited extra money to use for special occasions.

''It won't cost anything because I have passes.'' She pulled three tickets from her pocket and waved them in the air.

''Where did you get those?''

''From Tim.''

''As in Tim Carlton?''

''Yup. He works there.''

''And gave you free tickets. Just how many times have you met this guy for coffee?'' She eyed her sister suspiciously as she sat up straight. ''Come on. Out with the details.''

Peggy smiled rather shyly. ''I already told you how we ran into each other at the café. One thing led to another and now we're…well, we're sort of…'' She paused.

''Dating?''

Peggy had a silly grin on her face as she nodded excitedly. ''I've been wanting to tell you, but you know how I've never had much luck with guys and I wanted to make sure he was really interested in me before I talked about him.''

''He's obviously interested if he's giving you tickets for the museum.''

''Yes, he is,'' she agreed, her eyes sparkling at the thought. ''So will you come with us tomorrow? Tim's working.''

''Aha.'' That explained the reason for the trip to the museum. ''He's my age, isn't he?''

''A year older. He's twenty-five. After he was discharged from the navy, he lived in California for a while before coming back here.''

"And he's single?"

Peggy grinned. "He most definitely is. And he knows about Emma."

Marcie knew that dating had not been easy for her sister since Emma's birth. It hadn't taken Peggy long to discover that many guys her age weren't ready for an instant family. Even the most ardent suitors disappeared once they found out she was a single mom.

"He's nice, Marcie. And he's so good with Emma." She went on to extol his virtues and Marcie simply listened, pleased with the way her sister's face lit up as she talked.

"Sounds like the love bug may have bitten," she finally said with a sly smile.

She noticed Peggy didn't deny it. "He's so easy to talk to. When I'm with him I feel special."

"You are special."

"I'm also a single mom who lives from payday to payday and has student loans that it will take me years to repay," she said, slumping back in her chair.

"We've been through the worst, Peg. The future's looking bright."

She nodded. "I hope you're right. I haven't had much luck when it comes to guys. You know that."

"You know what Mom always told us. You have to kiss a lot of frogs until you find your prince," Marcie reminded her. That brought a smile to her sister's face. "Just take things one day at a time, Peg. And tomorrow, I'll come along if you want, okay?"

"Great. It'll be fun. You'll see."

And it was fun at the museum. Marcie enjoyed watching Emma try the science experiments designed for small children. She climbed up onto the locomotive engine and pretended to be running the train. She swung the long rope of the mariner's bell and watched the gears move on a giant clock. Curiosity mixed with laughter had her exploring the wonders of technology made basic enough for even a preschooler to understand.

Tim Carlton was exactly as Peggy had described him. Nothing at all like the scrawny kid Marcie remembered. When he was able to take a break from his work, he invited the three of them to get a treat at the ice-cream shop in the mall across the street.

It was obvious to Marcie that Tim was just as smitten with Peggy as she was with him. Marcie could see why her sister was attracted to the guy. Besides being nice to look at, he treated Peggy with a respect that had been sadly missing in her previous relationships and he had patience with Emma. Marcie sensed a genuineness in him that eased any concerns she had that Peggy was setting her cap for the wrong man.

While her sister took Emma to wash her hands, Marcie sat and talked to Tim. They compared memories of the old neighborhood where they had spent their youth, laughing over stories of pranks pulled by some of the more rebellious kids.

"You know, Marcie, I was really sorry to hear about your mother. If I had been here, I would have come to the funeral. She was one of the nicest people in the neighborhood," he said with a sincerity that touched Marcie's heart.

Even after five years, her mother's death could still bring a lump to her throat. "Thank you, Tim," she said, swallowing back her emotions.

He reached across the table to cover her hand with his. "It still hurts, doesn't it?"

She nodded. "Her death was hard for both me and

Peggy, but especially for Peggy. She was only sixteen.''

"She told me you put your own life on hold to become her guardian.''

"I did what any sister would have done. I'm very protective of her.''

He smiled. "Is that a warning?''

This time, she was the one who patted his hand. "I'm very happy you're dating my sister...you are dating, aren't you?''

His smiled widened and he chuckled. "I sure hope so.''

From the way Tim's eyes lit up with Peggy's return, Marcie couldn't help but feel a bit wistful. It had been a long time since a man had looked at her that way. Like Peggy, she wanted to find her prince. Yet there never seemed to be any time for romance. She was always working. And there was no chance for romance to happen at the office—especially not at the investment firm.

Her thoughts drifted to Jake Campbell. She knew he wasn't married, but maybe he had a live-in love. Not that it mattered. She wasn't interested in him. He was a hard, cold man. No, when she fell in love it would be with someone totally different from him. Once she stopped working for Jake, she'd never think of him again. Ever.

Jake hated shopping. He'd rather have teeth pulled than be dragged to the mall on a Saturday afternoon. Yet that was exactly where he found himself. And all because his sister insisted he come along to pick out the appropriate gift for their parents' wedding anniversary.

So to please his sister he had braved the traffic and

the masses of people toting shopping bags and pushing
baby strollers. One hour of elbowing his way through
the crowd was enough to ruin his disposition. As soon
as he and his sister had agreed upon the perfect clock
for his parents, he made arrangements to wait for her
in the mall while she completed the purchase and saw
that it was gift wrapped.

It was while he was waiting that he happened to
glance in the window of the ice-cream parlor. Seated
at one of the tables was Marcie MacLean. And she was
not alone. Across from her was a man.

It irritated him to see his prim and proper office temp
sitting in the ice-cream parlor with this brawny character. And what was worse, she'd let her hair down.
And it was glorious hair, tumbling to her shoulders in
big corkscrew curls. He couldn't believe what a difference a hairstyle could make to a person's appearance.
She was gorgeous. And sexy.

Wearing casual clothes, she looked much younger
than she did in the professional suits she wore to the
office. And her face was relaxed. Actually, she was
smiling at the blond guy seated across from her. When
she covered his hand with hers, Jake grimaced.

What he didn't want to see was Marcie holding
hands with another man. Why it should bother him, he
wasn't sure, but it did.

He moved so that the ice-cream parlor was no longer
in view. It was probably a good thing he had seen her
sitting there with her boyfriend. Several times during
the past week he had found himself wondering about
her personal life. Not a wise subject to contemplate.
She was, after all, his employee, and company policy
forbade any office romances. Fantasizing about Marcie
would not be wise.

That's why as he walked away he made a vow to himself that in the future he would only regard her as his assistant. Even if she did have glorious hair that could turn a man's thoughts to romance.

Although Marcie was thirty minutes early when she arrived at the office on Monday morning, Jake was already hard at work at his desk. Dark eyebrows edged toward the bridge of his nose when he saw her.

"I don't expect you to start early every morning, Marcie."

"I don't mind. There's a lot of work to be done."

"Yes, there is. Come in when you're ready to get started," he called out to her.

She was tempted to take a few minutes to catch her breath. So far, every day working for Jake had been grueling. He seemed to delight in testing her abilities, and though he'd not yet found a task she wasn't up to, the pressure was draining. She had to wonder if today would be any different.

"What do we do first?" she asked as she entered his office.

"We have to go over my notes for the tax seminar. There are handouts to be printed and you'll need to make sure I have the correct slides for the presentation. I'd also like you to confirm the travel arrangements for Chicago."

"Of course, but about the trip..." Marcie began hesitantly.

She'd been stewing about it ever since she realized that she'd be going away overnight with Jake. She had come to the conclusion that she couldn't go. There were too many reasons not to go—Emma being the main one. Peggy relied on her to share the child-care responsibilities. There was also her lack of appropriate clothing for such a trip. Everything in her closet was suitable for the office, but according to the restaurants listed on Jake's agenda, she'd need something dressier than a business suit.

However, the main reason she didn't want to go was because of Jake himself. He was a difficult taskmaster, making every day in the office exhausting. She could only imagine what two days in Chicago with nonstop business meetings would be like. It was one thing to function as the perfect assistant for a day, but forty-eight hours straight without a breather might be her downfall.

There was also the personal aspect. He was an attractive man—too attractive for Marcie's peace of mind. She found her anger and wariness toward him often disappeared with a smile and a wink. The man could turn on the charm when he chose and the very last thing she needed in her life was to become enamored of her boss—especially not when he was ready to fire her at the first mistake she made. No, traveling with Jake Campbell was definitely not a good idea.

"What about the trip?" His eyes narrowed as he asked the question.

"I won't be able to go to Chicago," she found the courage to say despite the thunderous look on his face.

"When you accepted this job, you agreed to be an administrative assistant, Marcie. Broken down into verbs, that means you must both administrate and assist. Need I remind you that you've already told me you would attend the conference?"

"I realize that, but it's not going to work out."

"Why? Are you having problems arranging child care? Is that it?"

"Not exactly, but Emma has been having trouble with ear infections and I'd rather not leave my sister alone with her just now," she answered honestly.

"If that's the case, I'll hire a nurse to stay with her."

She stared at him in disbelief. "You'd do that?"

"Yes, I would, Ms. MacLean, because that's how important this seminar is to me. I need an assistant with me. Once we get there, you'll understand why. Now if you're not going to be able to make it, tell me now and I'll arrange for someone to take your place."

He was issuing her an ultimatum. Go to Chicago or be replaced. Marcie knew that if there was one thing she couldn't afford, it was to lose such a well-paid assignment. Besides, she knew he was right. It was her job and she had told him she would do it. The problem was she hated feeling uncomfortable and that was a constant state whenever she was in the same room with him.

She'd just have to grin and bear it. Keep her chin up and pretend that he was just another temporary boss. She'd worked with plenty of attractive men in the past and had always managed to keep things in perspective. This trip to Chicago would be no different.

"I'll go," she said quietly.

"Very well, that's settled, then," he said in a very businesslike tone, then turned his attention to his work.

Marcie thought she needed to take a page out of his book. Learn to keep her emotions separate from her professional life. She had the job, she knew she was capable of handling the responsibility, and he was satisfied with the work she had done so far. There was no reason to be anxious.

So why did the thought of going to Chicago with Jake make her feel as if she were on a roller coaster and it was on its slow ascent to the top of a very steep drop?

"Let me put that away for you." Jake reached down to pick up her suitcase, then shoved it into the airplane's overhead compartment.

"Thank you." In the narrow confines of the plane it was necessary to jockey for position. She stepped aside in an attempt to avoid brushing up against his cashmere coat, but she couldn't prevent the contact. It made her skin all tingly.

When he offered her the window seat, she declined. She was determined not to be trapped against the wall of the plane unable to escape without virtually crawling across his lap.

She closed her eyes and pretended to sleep, but as soon as they experienced takeoff, he tapped her on the arm. Marcie flinched.

"Sorry to disturb you, but I'd like you to skim these notes so you can print up the changes as soon as we get to the hotel."

The hotel. To Marcie's mind he might as well have said "the dungeon" or "the torture chamber". Why she should be so wary made no sense. She had seen Brenda's notes regarding the hotel. Two rooms had been reserved—one for her boss, the other for her.

Only, either the proficient, unerring Brenda had prewedding jitters when she had made the arrangements or the hotel reservation system was flawed. When they arrived, there was no room reserved for Marcie, only a suite for Jake. He seemed unrattled by the error. She could feel her face grow warmer by the minute as the desk clerk went to great lengths to secure another room.

When it became evident that there were no more rooms available in the hotel, Jake told the desk clerk that Marcie could take the second bedroom of his suite. Without bothering to consult her, he checked them in and headed for the elevator.

"Shouldn't you have asked me if I would mind sharing your suite?" she asked as she followed him.

"It has two separate bedrooms, two baths. We're hardly sharing anything," he pointed out, which sent another flush to her face.

"But..." She trailed off, wondering how to bring up the subject of propriety. She didn't have to. He did it for her.

"There's nothing improper, Marcie. I've stayed at this hotel before, and when you see the size of the suite, you'll understand why it's not a big concern. No one at the conference is going to think you're anything but my assistant."

That did little to ease Marcie's mind. It felt rather illicit, which was ridiculous. He had given her no reason to think that he regarded her as anything but an employee.

Her nervousness must have shown on her face. As the elevator doors slid open, he whispered, "Relax, will you? The bellman's going to think you're frightened of me."

Which wasn't far from the truth.

Marcie gasped when the door to the suite opened. Never had she spent the night in such luxury. The parlor was done in shades of pale green from the damask silk, ceiling-high draperies to the exquisite settees and plush carpets. Fresh flowers graced the polished mahogany tables and she couldn't resist bending her head to sniff the fragrance of the closest bouquet.

"May I show you the suite?" the young man asked solicitously, taking for granted that the two of them would follow him. "The master bedroom."

The door swung open to reveal a room of dark burgundy and mahogany wood. A massive four-poster bed sat center stage, dwarfing the other antique furniture in the room. Marcie felt a little flip-flop deep and low in her body and she averted her eyes.

"The master bedroom has its own bath, of course, for privacy." Thank heaven for small favors, Marcie thought as the man went on. "And here is the second bedroom."

While the first bedroom was burgundy, the second was white, a vast expanse of ruffles and whitewashed furniture. Even the roses on the nightstand were white.

"It, too, has a bath, although not quite as large as the master. There is also another bath on the other side of the parlor, next to the bar." He efficiently explained the services offered by the hotel before saying, "Now, is there anything else I can do for you?"

Marcie thought she should speak up and say, "Yes, leave me a map so I can find my way around this place." She didn't belong in a hotel suite that she guessed cost as much for one night as her apartment cost for a whole month.

Jake seemed unimpressed by the surroundings and began to empty his briefcase onto the long mahogany conference table. He looked up to see Marcie, open-mouthed, watching him.

"You can set up the computer and check out the fax machine to make sure it's working. I'd appreciate it if you'd screen all calls. I don't want to be interrupted unless it's an emergency." Just as if he was in the office, he became all business.

There was nothing like hard work to make Marcie forget her surroundings. Several hours later she was regarding the posh suite as little more than a fancy prison.

Suddenly, Jake pushed back from the table and stood up. "That'll do it for now. Confirm the dinner plans for this evening and then you're free. We'll meet back here at six-thirty."

Before she even had time for her purposeful "Yes, sir", he had disappeared into the master bedroom.

Marcie made her calls, asked for a limo, tidied up the table and glanced around the room. Curious, she poked her nose into the bar to find it fully stocked. The bathroom next door was more of a powder room, with imported hand soaps arranged artistically across the vanity.

Exhausted, she headed for her bedroom. It was bigger than most of the apartments she'd lived in, Marcie decided as she unpacked her small overnight suitcase and put away her things. Never had she slept on such a huge bed and she couldn't resist plopping down onto it.

"So this is what money buys," she said on a sigh as her head sank into the luxurious softness of the pillows. She closed her eyes, thinking she'd rest for just a minute. When she opened them again, she realized that an hour had passed.

Not that it mattered. She still had plenty of time to take a bath before she needed to get dressed for dinner. She stripped bare and slipped into the fluffy white robe and slippers laid out for her by some diligent member of the housekeeping staff.

With her small bag of toiletries in hand, she headed for the bathroom. She opened the door and was surprised to find the light was on. She soon found out the reason why. In the tub filled with sudsy water was a very large man.

The squeak of alarm she gave didn't nearly cover the horror she felt at walking in on her boss, nude and soaking wet. She closed her eyes, dropped her bag and fumbled for the door.

It was futile. Marcie stubbed her toe on something porcelain and a sizzling pain shot up her leg. She let out another tiny scream.

"What are you doing?" demanded a voice that managed to shake her right down to the bones.

"I am so sorry. So sorry. So very, very sorry...." She shoved her hands out, feeling for balance and direction in a black world.

"For heaven's sake, open your eyes, Ms. MacLean, before you break both your big toes."

"But I can't, you're—"

"I've covered myself," he barked. "Didn't anyone teach you to knock before opening a closed door?"

She opened her eyes and discovered he'd pulled a fluffy white towel into the water, covering as much of him as possible. "I'm leaving," she said, then bent to retrieve the bag of toiletries. As she did, she noticed that the lapels of her robe had come open to reveal a generous amount of flesh. Surely he had noticed? Humiliated, she wanted to die. Unfortunately—or fortunately—one cannot die on command, so instead she tightened the belt and shot out of the room.

She didn't stop until she had found her own private space. She collapsed on the bed and pulled a pillow over her head. How could she have managed to do such a stupid thing? Why hadn't she noticed the layout of the double bathroom before? Why hadn't he roared at her before she managed to get so far into the room? Was all that muscle God-given or did he have to work out...? The pillow muffled Marcie's groan.

There was only one thing to do. Wash her embarrassment down the drain. And this time, she'd make no mistake as to which bathroom door she went through.

CHAPTER FOUR

MARCIE avoided looking at her boss as they rode to the restaurant in the limousine. That was because every time she did toss a glance his way, the memory of how he had looked sitting in the bathtub flashed through her mind and a warmth spread through her body. She wished with all of her might that she could just take back those few moments in time when she had pushed open the wrong door.

She was relieved that he hadn't mentioned the incident once, yet at the same time she wondered if she should say something to clear the air. Not that there was any time to talk. He made just as many calls from his cell phone as he did from his office, causing Marcie to wonder if there was ever a time when Jake wasn't doing business of some sort.

Although Marcie was experienced in making travel arrangements, as a temp she had never accompanied any of her bosses on a business trip. A knot of anxiety twisted inside her stomach at the thought of the evening ahead of her.

She was relieved to discover the dinner party was small enough that she didn't feel overwhelmed, yet large enough that she was able to sit at the opposite end of the table from Jake and have a conversation that didn't include him. She couldn't help but notice, however, that Jake Campbell, the host, was nothing like Jake Campbell, the boss. Marcie could see why he was the one to represent the investment firm at this important seminar. Not only was he brilliant with figures, but he was as smooth as silk when it came to selling the company to prospective clients and possessed a charm few people could resist.

By the time dessert was served, Marcie knew the evening had been a success. She finished her duties, settling the bill and arranging for taxis to take the guests back to their hotels. As soon as the last of them had departed, Jake gestured for her to get into the limousine.

"Very well done, Marcie." His voice came out of the darkness from his side of the car. "You were the quintessential assistant this evening."

"Thank you. I appreciate the compliment," she said, shifting uncomfortably. She had become quite accustomed to his criticism, but his praise…well, that caught her a bit off guard.

"Every man at the table made sure I knew what a gem of an assistant I had at my side. You impressed them—in more ways than one."

"I was just doing my job," she said modestly, trying not to let his words affect her. But they did. A warmth spread through her as his eyes studied her with an intensity she found disarming.

"You look lovely in that dress."

This time, the warmth became a flash of heat. The sparkle of appreciation in his eyes made her wonder if he was looking at her as a woman because of what had happened earlier. After all, she had seen more of her boss than any employee ought to see.

In an attempt to steer the conversation away from the personal, she said, "This is the first time I've ever been to Chicago."

"If the schedule wasn't so full, I'd offer to take you sightseeing."

She looked at him then. "That's not necessary. I came here to work, not be a tourist."

"Yes, this is about business, isn't it?" he said coolly, then turned to stare out the window. No other words were spoken until they arrived at the hotel. Then as they walked past the lounge, he asked, "Care for a nightcap in the bar?"

Marcie seldom drank alcohol and she had already had a glass of wine with dinner. So she declined his offer, not wanting to risk making a fool of herself for a second time that day. "Not for me, thank you."

Jake simply shrugged. "As you wish."

They rode the elevator in silence, an awkwardness stretching between them. Marcie knew the reason for her discomfort. Despite all the praise he had given her for her work that evening, what was foremost in her mind was the embarrassing incident that had occurred in his bathroom.

She needed to clear the air. Maybe he was able to pretend it hadn't happened, but she couldn't. When they reached the suite, she knew she could let it go no longer.

As soon as they were inside, she faced him. "Jake, I'd like to talk to you, if I may. About this afternoon—"

"Marcie, it's already put in the past as far as I'm concerned," he demurred.

She could feel her cheeks color. "Maybe, but unless I offer you a formal apology, I'll feel as if it's getting in the way of our professional relationship. I don't know how I mistook your bath for mine, but..." She paused to swallow back her humiliation, then added sincerely, "I'm really sorry. It was embarrassing for both of us."

"I was the one caught without any clothes," he reminded her. "Although judging by the frenzied way you were stumbling around, one would have thought it was the other way around. Surely you've seen a naked man before."

"Actually, I haven't…not that it's any of your business," she said stiffly.

"But you have a child."

"No, I don't."

"Emma, the little girl with the ear infections?" He looked at her as though she had to be the world's biggest dimwit to forget her own child's existence.

"She's my niece, not my daughter," Marcie explained.

For the first time since she'd been working for him, he looked totally taken aback. "Your niece?"

"Yes."

"I see."

Marcie wondered if he did. She was tempted to explain about Peggy and Emma, but then she remembered the advice Sandra gave all her employees. There was no reason to bring your personal life into the workplace. Jake was her boss, not her friend. The less personal information that passed between the two of them, the better.

Before another word was said, there was a knock at the door. Marcie watched as Jake went to see who it was.

Standing outside was a hotel employee with a linen-draped cart. "Room service."

"There must be a mistake. I didn't order anything," Jake told him.

"It's complimentary. From a Mr. Patterson," the uniformed man informed him, naming one of the guests who had been at dinner. "He wishes you to have a nightcap to celebrate the success of a job well done."

Jake stepped aside and allowed the man to push the cart into the room.

On it was a bottle of champagne on ice and two fluted glasses. The hotel employee looked at Jake. "Shall I pour, sir?"

"Yes," he answered, then turned to Marcie and said, "We might as well have a glass. It'd be a shame to let it go to waste, don't you think?"

Marcie wanted to say, "None for me, thanks." Her limited experience with champagne had shown her those little bubbles were able to destroy brain cells, popping them one at a time until she invariably did or said something stupid. And when it came to dealing with her boss, she definitely needed her wits about her.

Yet she didn't want to offend him, either. So she found herself saying, "Maybe just a little wouldn't hurt."

The last thing Jake had expected when he left the restaurant with Marcie was that they would end up sitting side by side on the sofa sipping champagne.

"To a successful dinner party," he said, lifting his glass in salute to hers.

"To success," she echoed, then swallowed the bubbly liquid as though it were water. By the way her eyes widened, he could see that the taste had caught her off guard. It was obvious she was unaccustomed to it.

"What do you think?" he asked.

In a manner he found charming, she licked her lips. "Hmm. This is good," she said with a shy grin.

"Yes, it is good, isn't it?" he agreed, thinking not of the champagne but the fact that the two of them were relaxing together without the pressure of work. A warning signal flashed in his head. The last thing he needed to be doing was unwinding with his assistant. Besides the fact that company policy forbade employees from getting involved in romantic relationships, he had his own personal code of ethics that included no socializing with employees after hours. Yet he was, enjoying Marcie's company and not wanting to see the night come to an end.

"You're very good at convincing people you know what's best for them," she said, studying the bubbles in her glass.

"Be careful, Marcie. That almost sounds like a compliment," he teased, liking the way the champagne had softened her prim and proper professional demeanor.

"Oh, it is," she said. "If I had any money to invest, I'd come to you."

They were small words of praise, yet Jake felt as if she'd just told him he was the smartest man on the face of the earth. "I appreciate the vote of confidence," he said, fighting the urge to touch her. Not for the first time that evening he wanted to reach for her hand, to feel its softness, to bring those fingertips to his lips.... As he poured more champagne, he said, "You surprised me today."

"Why is that?"

"Your familiarity with the bond market, for one thing. As efficient as Brenda is, she's not comfortable talking finances at dinner. You held your own very well. Anyone who didn't know you were my administrative assistant might have thought you were one of our market analysts."

"I've always been interested in finance," she told him. "Working for Sandra I've gained a lot of valuable experience."

"Which tells me the practical may sometimes be more advantageous than the theoretical," he observed. "Tonight you sounded more savvy about the market than some of my employees with graduate degrees from university."

"Just because I don't have a degree doesn't mean I'm ignorant of market trends." He could see she wanted to sound sanctimonious but only managed to achieve a charming flippancy that made him want to grin.

"No one could accuse you of being ignorant," he said indulgently.

"I'm not." She raised the flute to her lips and took another sip. "And I appreciate your vote of confidence, too." She looked at him then and giggled. "We sound like a mutual admiration society, don't we?"

He grinned. "A little. Do you have lots of admirers, Marcie?" he asked, knowing perfectly well that he was out of line. Her personal life was none of his business, yet ever since she had admitted that the little girl in the picture on her desk wasn't her daughter, curiosity about her private life had been nagging him.

"Most people think I do a good job," she responded, telling him that she thought he was referring to her employers, not the men in her life. She finished the champagne and set the glass down on the coffee table. "I should probably go to bed."

"Are you sure you won't have just one more glass? Champagne goes flat after it's opened and Mr. Patterson did spend a lot of money on this."

She bit down on her lip as she debated whether to

stay or go. Finally, she said, "All right, one more. But only one." As he filled her empty glass, she asked, "Do you and Brenda drink champagne together after a long day?"

He chuckled. "Hardly. Brenda is very predictable. At the end of a long day, she retires to her room to write follow-up notes to the guests we've entertained, polish her sturdy black pumps, and get a good night's sleep."

"Then perhaps that's what I should do."

"But you aren't Brenda. And I doubt you have any sturdy black pumps."

That made her blush. "You haven't seen my closet. My friends all think that if I ever wanted to start my own business I could open a shoe store with all of my cast-offs."

"I doubt those would find their way onto Brenda's feet. I've never seen her toes." He glanced down at the strappy little pair of shoes that made Marcie's ankles look slender and sexy. Again his brain flashed a warning. He was thinking of this woman as something other than his employee.

He changed the subject then, telling her anecdotes from past conferences that had her giggling and making him feel as if he were a fabulous storyteller. When she finally declared she must go to bed, he reluctantly helped her to her feet. It was only as she stood that he realized the champagne bottle was empty. Her wobbliness was a testament to the fact.

"Oh-oh. The bubbles did something to my legs," she declared with an innocence Jake found charming. It would have been so easy to forget that she was his employee, to respond to the slender, warm body leaning against his. "Do you know what wobbly legs mean?"

"Yes, I do. It's time for bed, Marcie." Just before she keeled over, he caught her in his arms and carried her into her room.

"Time for bed." Those were the only words Marcie could remember when she awoke with a start—and a pounding headache—the next morning. She breathed a sigh of relief to find she was sleeping in her own bed in the virginal white room—alone. She was still in her clothes of the night before but minus her shoes. Jake had obviously gotten her to bed and covered her with the fluffy down comforter. Her face felt tight and dry from yesterday's makeup and her hair was a lopsided mess of curls that had come loose from her chignon.

And she soon discovered she looked worse than she felt. As she walked to the bathroom, she passed the full-length mirror and gasped. Mascara ringed her eyes like a raccoon's. Her hair bristled more than her brush. And her dress could not be worn again without a serious meeting with a dry cleaner.

A groan slipped through her lips. How was she going to face Jake? What had she said or done? Had she blown her assignment so badly that he would fire her once again?

Then her practical nature took over. Ruined or not, she needed a shower. This time, stopping first to check for occupants, she entered the bathroom and punished herself with an extremely hot shower and a vigorous scrubbing. She felt almost human by the time she'd dressed, dried her hair and put on enough makeup to hide most of the ravages of the night before.

Jake was already dressed and seated at the conference table drinking coffee. The long mahogany table was set for two at one end. A basket of croissants, muffins and Danish sat next to the dinnerware.

"Good morning." He greeted her with a smile.

Marcie thought he looked amused.

"It *is* good, isn't it?" he asked when she didn't return his greeting right away.

"Marvelous!" The smile she gave him nearly broke her face as she joined him at the table. With her head feeling as if someone had climbed inside and was beating on every possible surface in an attempt to get out, she had no appetite for anything.

That's why she nearly had to excuse herself when Jake said, "If you'd like eggs and bacon or biscuits and gravy, just call room service. I usually don't eat much in the morning."

Marcie tried to avoid the sight of pastries and butter patties stamped with the hotel's insignia. She could see by the look on his face that her boss knew exactly how she was feeling and was amused by it.

After taking a sip of coffee, she said, "About last night…"

"What about it?" he asked with a lift of one brow.

"I didn't behave in a very professional manner and I want to apologize," she managed to say despite the pounding in her head. She avoided his eyes, focusing on the coffee he had poured for her.

"No apology is necessary," he told her.

She met his gaze then and saw that he was sincere.

"Our work ended at the restaurant. Just because we chose to unwind a bit after hours doesn't mean you're unprofessional, Marcie."

Unwind a bit? She was having a hard time recollecting what she had even said last night, but the simple

fact that she couldn't remember walking into her bedroom and knowing that she had slept in her clothes was
a source of embarrassment in itself.

"That may be, but I shouldn't have had so many
glasses of champagne. I seldom drink and I never drink
while working. Well, I guess I can't say never now,
can I?"

She expected he might make some glib remark, but
he didn't. He simply said, "I understand. There'll be
no more champagne."

Now that he had said exactly what she wanted him
to say, she felt disappointed. She had enjoyed last
night. He had been charming and witty—so unlike the
man he was in the office.

He glanced at his watch. "As soon as you've finished, we have to get to work. My presentation starts
in two hours."

And it's back to business as usual, Marcie realized.
Last night was of no consequence this morning. There
was only one thing on his mind. Work. Not once in
the next two hours did he even refer to what had happened and she was grateful.

Unfortunately, gratitude was a more uncomfortable
emotion than anger. Anger allowed her to keep her
distance from the man who'd been her nemesis.
Gratitude permitted other feelings to creep in. When
she was angry with him, she could think of him as not
having a heart. The minute he behaved in a benevolent
manner toward her, she was forced to admit there actually was a compassionate side to him.

It was safer to think of him as not having a heart.
She didn't want to be attracted to him, yet as much as
she hated to admit it, she was acutely aware of him as
a man. And if she was pressed, Marcie knew she would

have to admit to being attracted to her irritating, frustrating and absolutely gorgeous boss.

But it would never go further than that, she knew, because of the one thing she could not change. Her internship with Jake Campbell had nearly cost her the career she loved. He wouldn't forget and neither could she. Last night the champagne might have made her forget temporarily, but that would not happen again.

All she had to do was make it through the rest of the assignment without any more mistakes, collect her paycheck and go home. She would be vindicated and perhaps she could leave him feeling guilty about the devastating role he'd played in her life.

It wasn't that she was seeking revenge. It was not in her nature to be vindictive. No, she just wanted to show this man that he had been wrong to take such extreme measures. That's why she doubled her efforts to be the most efficient administrative assistant at the seminar. No one—not even Jake—could have found fault with a single thing she did the rest of the day.

They worked nonstop from the minute they left the suite until they returned late that night. True to his word, there was no suggestion of winding down at the end of the day with a nightcap. As much as Marcie wanted to feel relieved, she felt a bit disappointed. The after-hours Jake was a man whose company she enjoyed.

The entire trip was exhausting for Marcie and it wasn't until the following day that she was given a break from the hectic pace. Jake suggested she take an hour off to get a glimpse of Chicago. She took advantage of his offer and headed downstairs on her own, determined to at least get a peek at the city.

If there had been more time, she would have visited

the Field Museum of Natural History, but with only an hour to spare and having promised Emma she'd bring her something special, Marcie knew there was only one place to go—to the shops. Stopping at the concierge's desk in the hotel lobby, she picked up a street map and was about to head out the revolving door when she felt a hand on her shoulder. She turned to see her boss standing beside her.

"Wait up and I'll go with you," he said, tapping an envelope against his palm. "I just need to drop this off at the front desk."

"But I'm going shopping," she called out to him as he headed toward the desk.

"Good. So am I."

Marcie nearly groaned. He wanted to go shopping? Just when she thought she would have a little time to herself, he had pushed himself right back into her life. What she didn't need was for her boss to be breathing down her neck as she tried to browse the storefronts. Yet she couldn't tell him she didn't want him going with her. He was, after all, her employer.

When he noticed the map in her hands, he said, "You won't need that. I'll make sure you don't get lost."

Marcie folded the map in half and shoved it into her pocket and allowed him to escort her from the hotel. As he headed to the taxi stand, she said, "The concierge said I could walk to the mall."

"Yes, but that won't leave you much time to shop."

Even though she felt in need of some exercise, she knew he had a point. So she climbed into the cab.

"So what kinds of things are on your shopping list?" he asked when they'd reached the mall.

"Just one—a gift for a four-year-old."

"Your niece?" Seeing her nod, he asked, "Toys or clothing?"

"Oh, definitely toys."

As the taxi dropped them off, he placed his hand at her elbow. "If we go straight, we'll run into a great place to shop for kids," he told her, guiding her through the crowd.

"I don't want to keep you from your shopping. We can go our separate ways and arrange to meet when we've finished," she suggested.

"You want to deprive me of my opportunity to be a little kid. Is that it?"

She could see the humorous glint in his eyes. "No, it's just I thought you came along because you needed to do some shopping of your own and I didn't want you to think you needed to show me around this place. I think I can manage not to get lost."

"I'm sure you can and I appreciate your concern for my well-being."

Did she detect a hint of sarcasm in his response?

"But the truth is, I need to go to the toy store, as well," he added.

When he didn't elaborate, she asked, "You have to buy a gift?"

"Mm-hmm."

They had reached the store that Marcie discovered was actually two stories of the most incredible toys she had ever seen. She could see why Jake wanted to spend time in the shop. It was fascinating for both adults and children alike.

"Oh my goodness! I'm not sure where to even begin to look," Marcie commented.

The first thing they saw was an elaborate model-train display. Jake's eyes lit up as he watched the tiny trains zig and zag through tunnels and across bridges, and Marcie knew now why he had wanted to come to this store. Standing there mesmerized by the moving trains, he was like a little boy.

Together they admired the intricate layout until he said, "We'd better move on. What kind of gift do you want?"

"I thought I'd get her a stuffed animal—" He took her by the shoulders and turned her around. She gasped as she saw the menagerie of creatures before her. "There must be thousands of them."

"Why don't you browse here? I need to head over to the dolls."

That meant he was buying a gift for a little girl, too. "Maybe I should go with you. Emma loves dolls."

He led her by the hand as if *she* were a child. Actually, she felt like one, her eyes wide as they made their way to the doll section. As she expected, it was just as impressive as the stuffed-animal menagerie.

"You look a bit overwhelmed," Jake said as she stared at a display of dolls dressed in costumes from countries all over the world.

"I am." She slowly moved around the revolving carousel. "I never realized they made so many different kinds of dolls."

"Feel free to look around. I'll be in the area," he told her, then slipped down one of the aisles. So engrossed was Marcie as she continued to explore the huge assortment of dolls that she didn't realize how much time had elapsed until Jake said over her shoulder, "We're going to have to head back to the hotel in about ten minutes."

She noticed that he had a package in his hands. "You found what you were looking for."

"Yes. It's Vivien Leigh as Scarlett O'Hara. For my grandmother. She collects celebrity dolls."

Marcie had noticed the doll when they first stepped into the department and had thought it was beautiful. It was also very expensive.

"Is it her birthday?" she asked.

"No, it's no special occasion. She hasn't been feeling well lately and I want to give her something that will make her smile. She already has Clark Gable as Rhett Butler, so I have a feeling she's going to like this."

"I'm sure she will."

"I don't know where she's going to put it. I think every shelf in her house is full." He smiled fondly at the thought. "You ought to see her collection. It's incredible."

"I'd like to," Marcie answered, then immediately felt a bit foolish. What were the chances of her ever seeing his grandmother's doll collection?

As they stood there talking, she realized once more that away from the business arena, Jake was such a different man. He had patience, for one thing, and he smiled a whole lot more than he did while he was working. The fact that he bought his grandmother such a thoughtful gift for no particular reason other than to see her smile made Marcie look at him not as the monster who had fired her five years ago, but as a man she found to be very attractive.

"So which one are you getting for Emma?" he asked.

She had been debating between two dolls. Both were adorable babies, but one was twice the price of the other. Although she wanted to get Emma Baby Babbette and her pink layette, she knew it was out of her price range. Reluctantly, she picked up the other doll. "I'm going to go with Melody."

As she reached inside her purse for her wallet, he took the doll from her hands and set it back down. "I think this is a better choice," he said, picking up Baby Babbette. "Allow me." He took the doll and her layette and headed for the cashier.

She followed after him. "What are you doing?"

"Checking out," he said, handing the clerk the doll.

"But I'm not getting that doll."

"It's the one you'd rather have, isn't it?"

"Well, yes, but—"

"Then allow me to pay for it for you."

"I can't let you do that," she protested.

"Yes, you can. You've worked long, hard hours on this trip without once complaining. And you've worked with very few breaks. Think of this as a bonus for a job well done."

She wanted to object but was so overwhelmed by his generosity she couldn't get a single word to come out of her mouth. "Thank you," she finally managed to say as he handed her the package.

Marcie was uncomfortable the entire trip back to the hotel. She had it fixed in her head that Jake cared for nothing but his profit margins. Now she was seeing more and more of a tender side to him and she liked it. A lot. Hearing him speak so fondly about his grandmother made her wonder about the rest of his family. Was he close to them?

To her relief, it was business as usual once they were back at the hotel. He was his usual stern, demanding persona that made her wonder what had happened to that boy in the toy store.

She realized as he barked out orders that it was best

that she not see that little boy. What she didn't need
was to start thinking of Jake in a personal way. There
was no place for him in her life other than as a temporary boss. She would be wise to remember that. For
the sake of her job. For the sake of her heart.

CHAPTER FIVE

"WOULD you be able to stay late this evening?" It was a question Jake had asked Marcie often during the week since they had returned from Chicago. Not once had she complained about the long hours and he was grateful. That's why he was surprised when she didn't willingly agree today.

"It's Friday."

"Yes, which is why I need you to stay late. These reports need to be finished before the board meeting Monday morning."

"But everyone in the office leaves at three on Friday," she reminded him.

"Not everyone."

"Well, I'd like to." She straightened her shoulders. "I have plans for this evening."

"I'll pay you double time."

He could see she was tempted to accept his offer, but she didn't.

"I'm sorry, but I can't."

"Can't or won't?"

"Both."

He leaned back in his chair and studied her, liking the way she looked in her navy blue suit and crisp white blouse. Lately, she had been in his thoughts far too often, distracting him when he least expected it. With Brenda it was different. He hardly noticed her presence except when she spoke to him. But he was aware of Marcie even when she didn't say a word.

If it had only been the fact that she was pretty, she wouldn't be distracting him at all. But it was knowing that inside that beautiful head was a brain that loved the challenge of finance.

It was one reason he found her so intriguing. In the past she had been attractive, but her inexperience and lack of self-confidence kept him from thinking of her as anything but a bumbling intern. Now she was a smart and savvy woman with many facets to her personality. And he couldn't stop wondering about Marcie, the woman.

That was why when she said she couldn't work that evening he found himself annoyed. He didn't like to think of her having plans with a man, but he wasn't so foolish as to think she wouldn't have a boyfriend who wanted to go out on a Friday night.

"Must be a pretty special date if you're willing to pass up double time," he remarked.

"It's not a date. I'm doing my sister a favor," she told him. "And you said after the long hours we put in on the Chicago trip that you wouldn't ask me to work as many late evenings in the future."

Had he really said that? It must have been in a moment of weakness. Used to working long days, he often forgot that not everyone was as driven as he. And if she was doing her sister a favor...

"It's all right. You can go," he conceded.

"Are you sure?"

He wanted to say no. But how could he ask her to stay when she obviously had a family obligation? "Yes."

"Thank you. If you want, I could come in for a few hours tomorrow morning," she offered.

"You're willing to work on Saturday?"

"If you need my help, yes. You do work Saturdays, right?"

"Yes, but I normally don't come into the city. It's much more convenient to work at home. But if you're willing to come in, meet me here tomorrow morning...shall we say eight?"

"Eight is fine. I'll be here."

Deciding it might be wiser for him to take work home rather than stay late himself, Jake left shortly after Marcie. On his way to the garage he stopped at the newsstand on the main floor. As he purchased a paper, he saw his assistant on her way out the revolving doors.

He thought about following her and offering her a ride, but then he saw that she didn't need such an offer. Waiting for her outside the glass doors was the blond guy he had seen her with at the ice-cream parlor. As soon as the man saw Marcie, he smiled, then placed a protective arm around her waist as he ushered her into a red pickup in front of the building.

Jake's face twisted into a frown. *Some favor for her sister*, he thought as he tucked the newspaper under his arm and headed for the garage. And just when he thought Marcie could be trusted. He wasn't sure what bothered him more. The fact that she had lied or the thought of her in the arms of another man.

As he maneuvered his car out of the underground garage, he noticed the red pickup hadn't gone far, thanks to the bumper-to-bumper traffic. For several blocks, Jake's Porsche remained only a couple of car lengths behind the vehicle carrying Marcie and her guy.

When the pickup turned onto the freeway, Jake acted totally out of character and followed it. As much as he wanted to tell himself it was to check up on his employee, he knew that professional reasons weren't motivating his behavior. He simply wanted to see where she was going with this guy she claimed she wasn't dating.

"Thanks for picking me up today, Tim. That bus ride gets very tedious day after day," Marcie said with a grateful sigh.

"No big deal, Marcie. It's the least I can do. After all, your baby-sitting Emma allows Peggy and me to have some time alone." He gave her a wide grin. "And there's not enough I can do to thank you for that."

"You said on the phone you needed help picking out her birthday present," Marcie remarked, amused by the way Tim's eyes lit up at the mention of her sister.

"I do." Tim looked positively giddy at the thought. Marcie soon learned the reason why. "I want to give her a ring."

"Are you saying what I think you're saying?" she asked cautiously.

His grin was from ear to ear as he answered, "Yup. I want to ask her to marry me. And I remember her telling me that the two of you wear the same size ring."

"We do," Marcie said, a bit dazed by Tim's announcement, although she really shouldn't have been. She'd known from the first time she had seen her sister and Tim together that they had fallen in love.

"That's great. I hope you don't think that we're rushing things, but these past few months...well, they've been the happiest of my life."

"I bet Peggy would say the same thing."

"I sure hope so," he said eagerly.

"She hasn't had any easy life, Tim. And you're the

first man I've met that truly seems to love Emma as if she were your own. I'm very happy for both of you.'' Marcie patted him on the arm.

Tim's hand closed over her fingers. ''Thanks.''

Once they arrived at the mall they went directly to the jeweler's, where they pored eagerly over the selection of diamonds. As Tim tried to find the perfect ring, Marcie acted as a model, slipping them onto her slender, graceful hand. It didn't take long to whittle the choices down to three settings, which were both beautiful and in Tim's price range.

While Tim studied the loose diamonds, Marcie wandered off so that he could negotiate prices without feeling that she was prying. She meandered through the aisles looking at the rubies, sapphires, gold necklaces and the lavish settings. She admired the beautiful china settings and Waterford crystal knowing that it was unlikely that she'd ever own anything so lovely. She'd had to take out several loans over the years and it seemed that just as she paid off one, something came up that required another. Perhaps if Tim and Peggy married and she had only herself to support, it would make a difference, but Marcie had become so accustomed to being frugal that she couldn't imagine spending money so lavishly either now or in the future.

''Marcie, come here!'' Tim had moved to the front of the store with the clerk. He was holding a tiny gray, velvet box in his hand. ''I have something I'd like you to try on.'' As she neared, he opened the box and removed a lovely diamond in a delicate setting.

''Is this the one?'' Marcie leaned over his hand to study the ring. ''It is so beautiful.''

''Will you try it on for size?'' Tim asked eagerly. ''I want to see how it looks.''

"Of course." Marcie thrust out her hand, and with great solemnity and care, Tim slipped the ring on her finger.

From his vantage point outside the store, Jake could see the happy couple silhouetted in the window with the clerk standing at one side, his hands clasped in the pleasure of the sale. Jake watched every movement. The ring being lifted from the box, the willing offer of Marcie's hand, the satisfaction on the man's face as she admired the gem.

Jake wasted no time in returning to his car where his hands tightened on the steering wheel. With knuckles white and teeth gritted, he muttered to himself, "I guess it really is a family obligation when a woman wants to take a husband. But why not say it outright?"

He heard the gears grind as he thrust his car into motion and pebbles flew as he spun out of the mall. He opened the roof of the convertible and let the wind whip away any thoughts of Marcie.

By the time he reached home his temper had cooled and an icy resolve had settled in his chest. Somehow he'd allowed himself to succumb to those blue eyes and wild blond curls. Just because she had managed to efficiently fill Brenda's shoes didn't mean he should become infatuated with her—even if she did have a manner about her that teased his hormones.

This would be the end of that nonsense. There would be no more Mr. Nice Guy. From now on he would treat her as he had the first time she'd worked for him—with a critical eye and the impersonal clarity a boss should have for his employees. Jake had not achieved the success he had by surrounding himself with incompetents and with people who had the ability to rile him every time she—they—turned around. Nor had he ever forgotten the basic tenet of the office—never get involved emotionally with an employee.

Maybe it was a good thing he had seen Marcie's true colors this evening. At least now he could put away any romantic thoughts he may have harbored toward her. By the time he reached his front door, Jake's resolve was firmly in place. She was an employee—and a temporary one at that—and it was all she would ever be.

"Thanks for everything, Marcie," Tim said as he dropped her off at her apartment. "Now don't let on you know anything about this."

"Mum's the word," Marcie assured him. "I say nothing, I hear nothing, I see nothing."

"Good. I want this to be a big surprise for Peggy."

"I do too, Tim. She's due for a happy surprise in her life." Marcie gave his arm a gentle squeeze. "You're going to be a great brother-in-law someday."

In the apartment, Marcie picked up several of Emma's toys and tossed them into a laundry hamper designated for the purpose. Then she found a load of clothes in the dryer and proceeded to fold them. Tiny shirts, stockings with cartoon characters embroidered on the cuffs, and miniature blue jeans wrenched at Marcie's heart. She would miss her niece terribly once Peggy and Tim married, but she knew it was for the best. Emma and her mom both needed someone like Tim in their lives.

"And what about you, Marcie?" she said out loud. "What do you need?" She wouldn't have asked the question of herself if she'd known what might pop into her head. It was a vision of Jake, looking ever so handsome as he selected a doll for his grandmother at the toy store.

"Oh, no. Not that. Don't go there, Marcie old girl," she muttered. "You need another dose of him like you need another hole in your head."

Deciding she wasn't thinking clearly due to a lack of nourishment, Marcie began to put together a chicken potpie for supper—Emma's favorite—and complicated enough to make sure she banished the image of her boss from her mind.

"Anybody home?" Peggy called from the doorway.

"Just us mice," Marcie called back. She wiped her hands on the corner of her flour-streaked apron and held them out to Emma, who was launching herself out of her mother's arms and into her aunt's.

"Emma, sweetie, be careful. Auntie Marcie's cooking," Peggy chided as she watched her daughter plow into her sister. "What's for supper? Something smells wonderful."

"Homemade chicken potpie and a coconut cake."

"What got into you? A domestic streak the size of Georgia?"

"I just felt like keeping my hands and mind busy, that's all."

"Bad day at work?" Peggy asked sympathetically.

"You don't want to hear about my day, but I do want to hear about yours."

"Classes, homework, working at the café…same old grind." Then Peggy's features softened. "But Tim is taking me out tonight, so it's a great day!"

"You really care for him, don't you?" Marcie's heart warmed at the look on her sister's face.

"He's a wonderful man. Best I've ever met. He accepts Emma without a question. And he's smart and thoughtful and generous...and he treats me like a queen.'' Her eyes had that dreamy look Marcie was coming to expect whenever her sister spoke of her boyfriend.

"I agree. He's a very special man. You go and have a good time. Emma and I will feast on my culinary binge.''

"It smells good. Save me some?''

"Of course. You'll have lunches for next week. By the way, before I forget, I told Jake Campbell that I'd go in for a few hours tomorrow morning.''

"No problem. Emma and I can manage on our own.'' She glanced at her watch. "I better go get ready.'' Peggy was halfway to her room when she turned around and came back to give Marcie a hug. "You are the all-time, greatest big sister in the world, do you know that? You raised me and now you're helping me raise Emma. How will I ever thank you?''

"By being happy,'' Marcie said softly. "That's all I ask.''

"But are you happy?''

"Of course. I have my darling Emma to myself all evening. Now scram.'' But as Peggy was singing in the shower and humming as she did her makeup, Marcie thought about her sister's question. In many ways Marcie was happy. It had been a long time in coming, but she was almost out of debt. Her career was on a very nice track in the temp agency and Sandra was the world's best boss.

Marcie sighed. It was only her personal life that was a shambles. Or perhaps that was too strong a word. She really didn't have enough of a personal life for it to be a shambles. And therein lay the problem. For so long, all her free time had been spent with Peggy and Emma. It would seem odd not to have them around.

With another sigh, Marcie helped Emma wash up for dinner. Time passed slowly that evening as Marcie watched the clock, anticipating her sister's return and the jubilant celebration that would occur when Peggy showed Marcie her engagement ring. After putting Emma to bed, Marcie curled up on the sofa to watch a movie, determined to stay awake until Peggy returned, but she soon fell asleep.

When she awoke, it was midnight and her sister hadn't returned. When she'd left, Peggy had assured her that it would be an early night because she had so much homework to do. Of course, Peggy hadn't known about the ring or the kind of evening Tim had planned.

Shortly after midnight, Marcie ate three crackers and drank a glass of warm milk. When one o'clock rolled around and there was still no sign of Peggy, she went to bed, knowing that when her sister did come in, she would wake her up.

However, the next time Marcie awoke, it was to her alarm ringing. To her dismay, there was no sign of Peggy anywhere. Marcie tried not to worry, thinking that it shouldn't surprise her that her sister and Tim would want to stay up all night celebrating their engagement, yet she couldn't help but feel a knot of anxiety as she took a shower and dried her hair. Her worry increased when she dialed Tim's number and got no answer.

By the time Marcie had eaten breakfast as well as fed Emma, there was still no sign of Peggy. Marcie knew she was going to be late for work. Even though she knew how much Jake despised tardiness, she had no choice but to call the office and let him know she was running late.

While she was on the phone with her boss, Peggy, her hair disheveled and her eyes glowing, burst through the door. She halted when she saw Marcie in her business suit, the phone in her hand.

"Oh gosh, sis. I'm sorry," she said as Marcie hung up the receiver. "Tim and I had the most wonderful evening and we decided to see if we could see the northern lights, so we drove into the country. Oh, Marcie, it was beautiful and he asked me to marry him! It was so romantic I thought I'd die of pure happiness! We sat in the car and talked about our future and made plans to be a family, but we were both so tired because we'd been up so early yesterday that we fell asleep.

"He drove home as quickly as he could. I know I'm terribly late. Will your boss just kill you?" Peggy looked worried but radiant and Marcie's irritation melted.

"He sounded a little irritable, but he knows I had a good reason for being late." She spread her arms. "Now come give me a hug and show me that ring."

Peggy proudly displayed the diamond.

"Oh, it's beautiful! Congratulations! I'm so happy for you!" They hugged each other with such delighted abandon that they both nearly lost their footing. Emma, too, joined in the celebrating. "Okay. I must go," Marcie finally said. "I'd better call a taxi."

"No need. Tim's waiting outside to drive you to work. He feels terrible about this, too. He told me how you helped him choose the ring."

"Bless his heart." Marcie gave her sister and her niece one more hug, then waved goodbye.

Tim was as good as his word, waiting patiently by

the curb. He, too, was glowing. "Sorry, Marcie. It was a dumb thing to do, to fall asleep—"

"I haven't seen my sister this happy in years. Don't you dare apologize for anything. Just get me to work as quickly as possible without getting any speeding tickets, okay?"

Marcie thought he probably broke more than a few speed limits along the way, but she was still late for work. The thought of facing Jake was enough to give her goose bumps, yet she couldn't be angry at Tim. She had prayed long and hard for Peggy's happiness and she wasn't going to let a crabby boss spoil it for her.

As they came to a stop, Marcie leaned over and embraced her future brother-in-law. "Welcome to the family."

"Thanks." He returned the embrace with a big bear hug of his own, and when he released her, Marcie scrambled out of the pickup.

As she punched the up button on the elevator, Marcie wished wildly that it were a time machine that could spin back the clock.

Jake sat with a scowl on his face, his eyes on the clock at the bottom right-hand corner of his computer screen, wondering when Marcie would show up for work. He tried to concentrate on the pie-shaped graphs on the monitor, but he kept hearing her voice saying, "I can't leave Emma until Peggy gets home."

He wasn't such an ogre that he didn't understand that she had obligations to her niece and sister. But was it family responsibilities that had caused her to be late this morning? Last night she had said the same thing, that she was needed at home and couldn't work overtime. That had proved to be a lie.

He grimaced at the memory of her in the jewelry shop with her boyfriend. Marcie had turned down an opportunity to work with him to spend time with another man. He leaned back in his chair and sighed, wondering why this woman could twist his insides with so little effort. He was a man known for his composure in tight business situations, yet she managed to rattle him to distraction.

Jake pushed himself away from the desk and got up to stare out the window at the street below. On a Saturday morning there was little traffic. He watched as a city bus stopped at the corner. The doors opened; two women got off. Neither was Marcie.

He sighed. Where was she? He was about to turn away from the window when he noticed a red pickup stop at the curb. Jake had a hunch it was the same pickup he had followed last night.

His suspicions were confirmed when he saw Marcie climb out. It didn't take a Ph.D. to figure out where she had spent the night. Or the reason why she was late.

The knock on his door had him turning away from the window. "Come in."

Ed Batton from the legal department entered, grim-faced and carrying a file folder. "I heard you were in this morning."

"I've got a pile of work to do before the board meets on Monday morning...." He trailed off in explanation.

The man held up his hand. "I understand. I'm just glad you're here." He tossed the folder onto Jake's desk. "Take a look at that. We've got a problem."

It was true that Jake was a stickler for employees being on time, but he wouldn't have fired Marcie for being tardy on a Saturday morning, a day she shouldn't have had to even be at work. However, it wasn't her tardiness that was at issue. Ed Batton had seen to that.

"Come in, Ms. MacLean," he said when she poked her head around the door.

"You're angry," she said as a greeting, approaching his desk slowly.

"Do you realize what you've done?"

"I'm so sorry I'm late," Marcie began. "That family obligation I told you about yesterday—"

"Has nothing to do with this," he finished for her.

"Do with what?" He thrust the quarterly account summary of one Jason Farrell into her hands. She scanned it and gave him a puzzled look. "What's wrong? Did we miss one of his investment accounts? If so, I'll check into it right away."

"Oh, no, nothing's missing. Every penny of every fund is accounted for. Unfortunately, he's not the one who received this information," he said, barely managing to control his temper.

She gave him a perplexed look. "I don't understand."

"Who was in charge of the mailings this quarter?"

"I was. But it was handled just as it is every quarter. I checked protocol to make sure it was. Is there a problem?"

"And who is in charge of change-of-address notices in this office?" he demanded.

"I am. There's a file that I used to record changes to be keyed into the computer before the summaries are printed."

"And did you do that this month?"

"Yes. There were quite a few changes, in fact. More than I expected there would be."

"And did you have them double-checked by someone in the office?"

"Double-checked? Is that procedure?"

"You tell me." Jake thrust a letter into her hands.

"What?" She read the letter and gasped. "I sent it to the wrong Farrell?"

"Yes. Joan Farrell—the soon-to-be ex-Mrs. Farrell. They're legally separated and she is no longer on his account, which means she has no right to see his personal financial statements nor does he want her to see them. Do you realize what legal ramifications could result from such an error?"

She didn't reply but simply shook her head.

"Mr. Farrell requested specifically that it not be mailed to his former address but to his office."

Marcie looked at the address on the statement. It was a home address in a wealthy section of the city. "I don't understand how that could have happened."

"Neither do I. I was hoping you could tell me. You *were* in charge, Marcie. It was your job to update that list."

"But I did update it!"

"Then how did this happen?"

"I don't know, but I know I'm not responsible. If the change had come through for Mr. Farrell, I would have made sure it was entered correctly." Blue eyes looked up him, pleading for him to believe her.

He probably would have if she hadn't lied about her plans for last night. And about the reason for her lateness. And about not having a boyfriend. It would have been so easy to give her a chance to prove that she wasn't at fault in the Farrell mishap, but the memory of her walking arm in arm with the blond guy refused to allow him to be lenient.

"I'm going to call Sandra O'Neill at Temporarily Yours on Monday."

"You're letting me go?" she squeaked.

"I'll make sure you receive the pay you've earned."

She backed away, looking as if she wanted to cry, her teeth tugging on her upper lip. "I'll collect my things," she said in a shaky voice and left the room.

Jake thought he would be relieved. There was no place for dishonesty in his office. So why did he feel like such an ogre?

As Marcie stumbled back to her desk, she fought back the tears. She wouldn't cry. She wouldn't. But no matter how many times she repeated the words, she could feel the pressure building behind her eyes. She had to get to the ladies' room before she made a complete and utter fool of herself.

It was while she was splashing cold water on her face that Alicia entered.

"Are you okay, Marcie?"

"Umm—yeah, I'm fine," she said, then hiccuped. "What are you doing here on a Saturday?" she asked, trying to focus on the other woman.

"The same thing you are. Putting in overtime." She eyed Marcie curiously. "Are you sure you're all right?"

Marcie glanced in the mirror and saw big red splotches on her face. There really was no point in lying.

"No, I'm not. I was just fired."

"You? Miss Efficiency? No way!"

The whole miserable story spilled out of Marcie

then, about the dreadful error, about her complete blank about anyone named Jason Farrell and about the disappointment Sandra O'Neill would feel when one of her most trusted employees caused such a blunder. Alicia said nothing but frowned unhappily throughout Marcie's soliloquy.

Finally, Marcie collected her wits about her the best she could and excused herself. As unpleasant as it was, she needed to return to her desk and clear out her things. To her relief, when she got back, Jake was not in his office.

She worked quickly, not wanting to be there when he did return. A sick feeling gnawed at her stomach as she thought about having to face Sandra. And then there was Peggy…this was exactly the news she didn't want to bring home on what was such a happy occasion for her sister.

She was just about to leave when Jake entered the executive quarters. The minute Marcie saw him, she froze in place. The expression on his face was grim, making her legs feel as if they would crumple beneath her. Now what? Another scathing tongue-lashing? To her surprise, however, his voice was gentle when he spoke.

"Would you come into my office, please?"

She should have said she wasn't a glutton for punishment, and left. She didn't. She followed him into his inner sanctum and took a seat when he gestured to a chair.

"I've learned some new information since we spoke this morning," he began, standing next to her instead of sitting down in his leather chair.

"I owe you an apology. You're not to blame for the Farrell mishap."

As hard as she tried, she couldn't keep her mouth from dropping open.

"It was Brenda's mistake, not yours." Gone was the steely hardness that had been in his eyes earlier. In its place was a warmth she had only seen on a couple of occasions.

"How did you find out?"

"Alicia checked the files and found Brenda's initials on the data entry, yet the information hadn't been keyed into the computer. Maybe she was distracted by love...I don't know. But she certainly wasn't her usual efficient self those last few days before she left."

Marcie felt as if a great weight had been lifted off her chest. She wasn't sure what to say. It was as if she'd been tried and found guilty for a crime she hadn't committed only to be granted a pardon.

"You may stay on in your present capacity if you wish," Jake continued. "Of course, that is, if you accept my apologies."

She should have been grateful. He was giving her another opportunity, a second chance. But the truth of the matter was that he had jumped to the conclusion that she was to blame without so much as investigating what had happened. Just as he had done five years ago.

"Do you want to stay on?" he asked.

Marcie thought it would serve him right if she told him to take his job and shove it. Just let him spend the remaining weeks of Brenda's absence trying to train another temp.

Of course she didn't. She couldn't. Mainly because she needed the money, but also because, as much as she hated to admit it, she liked working for him. Being his assistant was the most intellectually stimulating job she had had in a long time and she enjoyed the challenges he presented.

She lifted her chin and said, "Yes, I'll stay. However, I would appreciate your giving me the benefit of the doubt in the future. I've worked here for over three weeks and have given you no reason to think I would do anything to jeopardize the success of this firm."

Marcie didn't expect him to be apologetic, but she did expect more than a shrug and a "Very well" from him.

"Would you still like me to work this morning?" she asked, rising.

"Yes. There is one other thing, however, before you start."

She glanced at his hardened features and felt herself tense.

"About this morning...you should know that this firm places a high value on arriving to work on time."

"I realize that and I can explain—" she began, only to have him cut her short.

"*Family obligations*, correct?"

"Actually, yes. You see, Emma was—" Again he interrupted her by raising both hands in the air, palms outward.

"Your personal life is your own, Marcie. I don't need to hear any of the details again. You were late. That's all that concerns me. If it happens again, I will call Sandra and request a new temp. Understand?"

"Yes," she said quietly. "I won't be late again."

"Good. Now, if you could make sure I have a copy of the board-meeting agenda..." he said, dismissing her without a second glance.

CHAPTER SIX

MARCIE was grateful that meetings kept Jake out of the office much of the following week. His absence, however, didn't keep him from making sure that she had plenty of work to do. By the time Friday afternoon rolled around, she was feeling exhausted and ready for a break from the responsibilities of being his assistant.

She was putting away her things and getting ready to go home when Jake stopped at her desk. He wore a tailored suit and pristine white shirt. Unlike the rest of the firm's employees who took advantage of the opportunity to "dress down" on Fridays, he looked as professional as he did every other day of the week. And just as attractive.

"About tonight..." he began.

"What about it?"

"I could send a car for you, but it might be better if I pick you up myself."

"Pick me up for what?" she asked, totally bemused by his assumption that she knew what he was talking about.

"The award dinner this evening. Didn't you read the memo I left for you?"

Marcie stared at him blankly. "You wrote me a memo?"

"Yes, and I set it on your desk. I'm sure I did," he said, giving her workplace a thorough scrutiny.

"I didn't see it," she admitted, noting that her basket for incoming work was empty.

Dark eyebrows drew together. "Then you have no idea what I'm talking about, do you?"

She shook her head. "I'm sorry."

"There's this award banquet…it's an annual thing. Normally, I'd ask Brenda to accompany me, but she's not here." He gazed at her hopefully.

"You want me to go?"

She tried to hide her surprise but knew she had failed when he said, "You *are* my assistant—at least for now."

"Yes, but…" She searched for an appropriate excuse but found her mind was blank.

"I realize that it's short notice."

"Yes, it is," she said, enjoying what appeared to be a crack in his usually stoic manner. She could see that he wasn't confident she was going to say yes and it bothered him.

"Are you available this evening?" He pinned her with a gaze meant to intimidate.

"I wasn't planning on working late this evening…" She paused deliberately before adding, "But I guess I can if it's important. What time is it and how long will it last?" She didn't want him to think she thought of their evening together as anything but a work-related arrangement.

"Cocktails are at seven, followed by dinner and the program. I expect it should be over around eleven."

"That late?"

"Is it a problem?"

"No." She didn't know why she was acting as if it was a big inconvenience. "If you give me the name of the hotel, I'll take a taxi and meet you there."

"That's not necessary. I can pick you up."

She'd get to ride in the Porsche. It might not be a

date, but it would certainly feel like more than a business arrangement. "All right," she heard herself say.

"Shall we say six o'clock?"

"Six is fine."

"Good." He started to leave, then stopped. "By the way, I should tell you it's a formal affair. You'll need to dress accordingly."

As he disappeared back into his office, Marcie felt a moment of panic. Nothing in her wardrobe could be classified as formal. Peggy did have one black dress she could borrow. It was a slinky, swirly thing her sister called her "wow 'em" dress because on the few occasions she had worn it, men had been wowed by her appearance.

Marcie mentally scolded herself. She didn't need to wow any man this evening and certainly not her boss. This was an assignment for which she'd be paid overtime. It would be no different from the dinner party she'd attended in Chicago except she and Jake would be dressed more formally.

The thought of seeing him in a tuxedo sent a tingle of anticipation through her. The last time she had been with a guy wearing a coat with tails had been her high school prom. At seventeen she had sighed dreamily at the sight of her date coming up the front walk in his rented tuxedo, prompting her mother to say, "Put any man in a tux and he becomes a prince."

Even without the tux, Jake was handsome enough to be a prince, Marcie acknowledged. Not that she should be having such thoughts about him. Besides the fact that he had falsely accused her not once, but twice of mistakes she hadn't made, she was quite certain there were already enough women willing to let him be a prince. To her he was simply her boss and that was all he'd ever be. Tuxedo or no tuxedo.

So why did her heart flutter at the thought of an evening with him?

"Don't you look nice!" Peggy said as Marcie entered the living room in her slinky black dress.

"Nice? She looks fantastic!" Tim added. "Peggy, if that's your dress, how come I haven't seen it on you?" he asked his fiancée.

"You will when it's the right occasion," Peggy answered, then turned her attention back to her sister. "I think it fits you better than it does me."

"I appreciate your letting me borrow it, but I'm not sure it's what I should be wearing tonight," Marcie said, uncomfortable with the amount of skin the tiny straps and plunging neckline revealed. "This is a professional function."

"It's a formal award dinner. That means all the women will be dressed to the nines," Peggy assured her.

"It just feels so...so...skimpy. Maybe I should take a shawl."

"You are not wearing one of Mom's old shawls," Peggy stated in no uncertain terms. "The dress is perfect, isn't it, Tim?"

"I'll say," her fiancé agreed. "You're going to knock 'em dead, Marcie."

"I don't want to be the center of attention. I just want to look as if I belong at a rather formal dinner," Marcie said, trying to still the anxiety that caused her hands to tremble.

"Trust me, you will," Tim said. "Every man in the room is going to think you belong."

"But what will my boss think?" she pondered aloud.

"From what you've told me about Jake Campbell, I'd say that dress is exactly what you need to put the man in his place," Peggy insisted. "I can't wait to see the look on his face when he sees you."

"You're not going to," Marcie told her. "I'm meeting him downstairs."

"What?" Peggy threw her hands to her waist in protest.

"This isn't a date, Peggy. It's business," Marcie said as she picked up her tiny cocktail purse. "I better go. Don't wait up for me." She blew them a kiss, grabbed her coat and was gone.

Jake pulled up to the curb just as she stepped outside. She hurried down the steps and tried to reach the Porsche's passenger door before he could open it for her, but he was too quick. Acting like the perfect gentleman, he helped her into the car, making sure she was comfortable before closing the door.

"Thank you," she murmured, wishing the simple gesture didn't make her feel as if they were on a date.

As he walked around the front of the car, she couldn't help but notice what a fine figure he made in his tuxedo. Her mother was right. The average man became a prince in a tuxedo. Only Jake wasn't the average man. He was tall, broad-shouldered and staring at her as if she was someone special he couldn't wait to take to dinner.

When he slid into the Porsche beside her, his musky cologne tickled her senses and made her think that the scientists who claimed sexual attraction began with scent were correct. His was attracting her like pollen signals a bee.

"You look lovely this evening," he said in a husky voice that sent little shivers of pleasure up and down her flesh.

"Thank you," she managed to say although her mouth was as dry as cotton.

He's your boss, a little voice in her head reminded her. *This is not a date.* She needed to keep the evening on a very professional basis, which is why she asked, "I'm assuming I'm getting time and a half for to-night?"

She saw him stiffen. "Yes, you'll get overtime pay," he said flatly as he pulled out into traffic.

Gone were any traces of the smile he'd bestowed upon her when he first saw her coming down the apartment steps. He no longer even glanced in her direction, let alone looked at her as if she was someone special.

Tired of the uncomfortable silence that stretched between them, Marcie finally asked, "So what kind of awards will be given out at this dinner?"

"Tall ones. Gold with a wooden base," he answered.

"That was an impressively obtuse answer. Are they business awards?"

"In a way," he said evasively.

Deciding that he didn't want to talk and since she wasn't really in the mood for idle conversation, she sat quietly as he drove. When they reached the hotel, he maneuvered the Porsche under a canopied entrance. One valet came to escort Marcie out of the car while another was there to spirit Jake's car away. From that moment on they were treated like royalty.

Inside the ballroom there was someone to take her coat, to get her something to drink, to offer her an arm, to shower her with compliments. Jake was the central attraction, with people rushing to greet him, oftentimes nudging Marcie out of the way until she finally grew tired of the jostling and stepped aside. She was content to stand back and watch from a distance as he charmed everyone clamoring for his attention.

It never ceased to amaze Marcie how differently he behaved when he was away from the office. Which was why it was dangerous for her to accept assignments like this evening. The charismatic Jake was very intriguing.

When she noticed him searching the room for her, she reluctantly pushed her way back to his side just as his brows began to furrow in the manner they did when he was frustrated or angry. He discreetly pulled her aside and asked, "Where did you run off to?"

"I didn't run anywhere. I was pushed away by your adoring fans. I thought I'd be trampled and you'd find me flattened, as if a steamroller had squished me into the road."

"Very dramatic but highly unlikely," he said next to her ear, his hand at her elbow. "Stick close to me from now on. I don't want to lose you."

I don't want to lose you. How lovely it would be to have a man say those words to her for all the right reasons—because he cherished her and couldn't bear to have her far from him. Jake, however, was watching over her the way he'd watch over a new puppy—making sure it didn't get hurt or into trouble. He was, after all, her employer and undoubtedly felt responsible for her.

A few moments later he said, "There they are. Come this way." He steered her toward the entrance to the ballroom where a small group of people stood waving vigorously and smiling in Jake's direction.

"Marcie, I'd like you to meet my parents, my grand-mother, my sister Caroline and her husband Tom," he said, introducing her to his family.

Marcie managed to say a few social niceties despite being caught totally off guard by their presence. They were warm and friendly and eager to talk about Jake, which she noticed made him a bit uncomfortable. It was obvious he cared for them deeply, indulging his parents' need to boast of their son's accomplishments.

He looked relieved when the announcement was made that everyone should move into the ballroom for dinner. Jake put a hand on Marcie's waist and gently urged her forward. The door opened with a flourish and she stared in at the rows of tables covered with white linen, fine china, crystal, silver and the most magnifi-cent floral bouquets she had ever seen.

What shocked her the most, however, was the huge banner over the podium on the speaker's dais. In bold blue letters it read Jake Campbell, Man Of The Year.

Marcie gasped, suddenly understanding why his family was at the dinner. "This banquet is for you!"

"Did I ever say otherwise?" Jake answered calmly, continuing to acknowledge familiar faces as if he were a seasoned politician working a crowd.

"But this is too special! I shouldn't be here," she protested. "I'm only your temporary assistant."

"Who's worked very hard. Besides, I want you here," he said in a voice that sent shivers up and down her spine. "Now smile and pretend you aren't sur-prised. I don't think it would look good if my admin-istrative assistant disagreed with their choice of Man of the Year, do you?"

It was like a dream, Marcie thought later—the food, the champagne, the accolades. She felt as though she was in the presence of a celebrated hero, not the man who seemed dead set on firing her for one sin or another. She listened as his accomplishments were described to the audience and found she had to fight the temptation to let her jaw drop open.

One by one, businessmen, political figures and civic leaders stood up and paid tribute to him with a sincerity that touched Marcie's heart. She learned more about her boss in thirty minutes than she could otherwise have managed in weeks of research.

He'd grown up the youngest of a large family and made his mark early on as a tenacious entrepreneur, setting up a lemonade and cookie stand outside a factory. Thanks to his mother's excellent baking and his determination to be of service to people, he had turned a small refreshment stand into a chain of lemonade carts that serviced local businesses and sporting events.

Jake had paid his own way through college and graduate school and never forgotten any of the people who helped him along the way. Besides his community work and generous contributions to charity, his benevolence continued to improve the lives of many youngsters, allowing them the opportunity to work for scholarships at one of the many Jake's Lemonade Stands that still traveled the city streets.

Marcie could see that Jake was uncomfortable with the praise, but the more she listened, the more her respect for her boss grew. Entrepreneur, civic leader, philanthropist, humanitarian. No one seemed to have a bad word to say about him.

Finally, when the accolades were over, it was Jake's turn to speak. Gone was the hard-edged businessman Marcie saw every day at the office. As he graciously accepted the honor that had been bestowed upon him, she could see that everything they said about him was true. With a modesty that Marcie found endearing, he eloquently thanked everyone and paid tribute to his family in a speech that had everyone rising to their feet at its finish.

After the handshaking and congratulations ended, Jake's family gathered around him. Marcie would have liked to excuse herself, but his father didn't give her the opportunity.

"I think we've heard from just about everyone tonight except the one person who spends more time with Jake than any of us. What about it, Marcie? Do you want to tell us what really goes on in Jake's office?"

Marcie's heart jumped into her throat. "I—"

Jake gave her a nudge, pushing her closer into the family circle, saying, "Here's your chance to say what kind of boss you think the Man of the Year is. You've got plenty to say when you want to...so go ahead."

"Well..." She paused. Jake was looking at her with a challenge in his eye, as if he dared her to tell the truth, to say what was really on her mind. The question was, could she?

Before she had a chance to say anything, however, his mother said, "Marcie, I hope he doesn't make you work through lunch. He can get so caught up in a project that he often forgets to eat."

"That's because once he has his mind set to do something, he doesn't stop until he's finished," his sister Caroline explained. "He's always been that way, but you mustn't let him bully you, Marcie. Beneath that tough exterior there's a soft touch."

It was something Marcie would have liked to see for herself. If only she could be the recipient of one of those affectionate gazes he tossed so frequently at his family members.

"I never bully, do I, Marcie?" The smile he gave her was full of the same teasing spirit that underscored his words.

"Well..." She grinned and raised her eyebrows, causing laughter among the group.

"It's all right, Marcie," Mr. Campbell said with a fatherly pat on her shoulder. "You don't need to incriminate yourself. We all know that Jake works hard and expects everyone around him to do the same." The words weren't said with criticism, but with pride.

"Yes, he does work hard, but I can keep up," Marcie assured them.

"She can," Jake agreed. "I used to think no one could come close to being as efficient as Brenda, but that was before Temporarily Yours sent me Marcie."

It was a compliment she hadn't been expecting, and she didn't want it to affect her the way it did, but she couldn't stop the blush of pleasure that spread over her body. Worried that he might see how much his praise meant to her, she said in a lighthearted aside to his family, "Obviously, he didn't feel that way when he fired me." She tempered the words with a wink.

"Fired you?" both his mother and sister echoed in unison.

Then Caroline said, "Is there a story here that we should know about?"

Suddenly wishing she hadn't brought up the subject, Marcie said, "It was nothing. Honest." She shrugged uneasily.

"It must not have been if you're with us tonight," Mrs. Campbell said with a warm, reassuring smile.

"Misunderstandings happen to all of us at one time or another."

Marcie met Jake's eyes then and said, "Yes, they do, don't they?"

"Why don't you just tell my mother the truth? That I made a mistake and misjudged you," he said, a hint of a challenge in his eyes.

"So you did fire her?" Caroline persisted.

"*Almost* fired," Jake corrected.

It was obvious to Marcie that her boss had conveniently forgotten about the first time he had let her go. She was tempted to remind him, but she knew this evening was neither the time nor the place to dredge up the past.

So instead she said, "It's true," producing a gasp from Caroline. Marcie quickly added, "But he did apologize."

Caroline's indignation disappeared with a smile. "Now *that* sounds more like the brother I know. If nothing else, Jake is a fair man. And I don't think you need to worry about my brother making that mistake again, Marcie," she added confidently. "The way he's been singing your praises to me, I'd say Brenda better mind her p's and q's."

Marcie held up her hands defensively. "Brenda's job is safe. I'm just a temp, remember?"

"You're more than that, Marcie," Jake said with a smile that nearly melted every bone in her body.

Fortunately, no one noticed her dreamy-eyed state as everyone's attention was drawn to the man at the speaker's dais who was making the announcement that the party was moving into the adjoining ballroom. As another set of doors opened, the crowd gradually made its way to the dance floor.

Marcie didn't know what to expect from her boss. Would he want to leave now that the presentation portion of the program was over?

To her surprise he pulled her by the hand into the ballroom and onto the dance floor. "Keep moving," he whispered. "It's less crowded out here."

Indeed it was. Because of the size of the ballroom, there was plenty of room for couples to dance without fear of bumping elbows. With the lights low and the music soft, she didn't find it difficult to relax and enjoy the experience.

Jake was not a shy dancer. His body moved in rhythm with hers, their thighs brushing, their bodies curving together as one. It was as if he caressed her with every step he took, which was why it became increasingly difficult to think of him as her boss.

She wondered if he felt the same way—that they were no longer boss and employee, but man and woman. His body was so in sync with hers that she felt as though he could predict her every movement. She lifted her head to look into his eyes, hoping to see if he was as affected by their closeness as she was, and her breath caught in her throat. What she saw there left little doubt that being with her was just as exciting to him as it was to her.

As he pulled her closer to him, she knew it was dangerous to allow herself to forget why she was with him, but all she wanted to do was enjoy the sensation of being in his arms. As he guided her across the dance floor, she allowed herself the fantasy of pretending that he was a real date. For tonight only, she would let him be a handsome man and herself his special lady. She'd worry about tomorrow when the music stopped playing.

"You have a nice family," Marcie told Jake as he drove her home.

"Does that surprise you?"

"No."

"Liar."

"All right, so I wasn't expecting them to be so friendly," she admitted.

"Then you do think I tend to bully my employees."

"No, but sometimes you forget that we're only human," she said quietly. "And that we occasionally make mistakes."

"I don't expect you to be perfect, Marcie. Didn't I apologize when I discovered I'd falsely accused you in the Farrell case?"

It was a question he didn't expect her to answer and she didn't. He was glad. He didn't want to talk about work, which is why he asked, "Did you enjoy this evening?"

"Yes, it was a wonderful party. I'm glad you included me in your celebration. Now I understand why you wanted me there. It would have looked odd if your assistant hadn't attended a dinner honoring your professional accomplishments."

"That's not the only reason I invited you," he said. He wondered if he should tell her what the other reasons were. As tempting as it was, he chose not to tell her that he had been looking for an excuse to date her and tonight had been the perfect one. "You know what thought kept running through my head this evening? I kept thinking this woman at my side can't possibly be the same woman who worked for me five years ago."

"I was young back then...very young," she said, a hint of regret in her voice.

"Yes, and I should have realized that," he admitted,

wishing that he could erase what had happened when she was an intern.

"Does that mean you wouldn't have fired me?" she asked.

He wanted to say yes, but the truth was he no longer was sure what he would have done. "Why talk about the past? We can't change what's happened."

She didn't heed his request. "Does it bother you that you fired me back then? I noticed you conveniently forgot to mention it when the subject came up in the conversation with your family."

"That's because I was trying to spare you the embarrassment."

"Well, thank you, Mr. Campbell, for being so considerate of my feelings," she said with a good dose of sarcasm. "I would have appreciated some of that concern when I was falsely accused of misusing e-mail privileges."

"Falsely accused? Marcie, you were the only one with access to your mailbox," he reminded her.

"That's the way the system was designed, yes, but that doesn't mean someone else couldn't have found out my password and used my mailbox," she contended.

"And how would that have happened?"

"I told you. I was young...and naive."

"Are you saying you *gave* your password to another employee?" There was a long silence that he ended by saying, "You did, didn't you?"

"Yes. One of the other girls in the office was in a bind and needed to do some research on the Internet and write a paper. She didn't have time to use the computer lab at school, so she wanted to do it on her lunch hour."

"She didn't have her own password?"

Marcie shook her head. "No, not for the Internet."

"So you let her use yours?" He tried to keep the disbelief from his voice, but he knew by the way she stiffened that he'd failed.

"Sharon and I were good friends. She was in a similar situation to mine. Her mother was ill, she was trying to finish school and at the same time help with expenses at home. I knew how stressful that was and I thought she was a responsible person—that she wouldn't do anything but a quick bit of research, print out her paper and be done."

"But obviously she didn't."

"No. I didn't realize it at the time, but she accessed my mailbox and read confidential correspondence. The rest you know."

"She copied it and passed it on," he concluded soberly. "Why didn't you tell me this then?"

"I tried to, but you wouldn't give me a chance to explain anything. Plus I shouldn't really have given her my password anyway. You would probably still have let me go."

He knew that what she said was true.

"Besides," she continued, "I couldn't prove I was innocent without incriminating Sharon. I knew how devastating it would be for her if she lost her job, with her mom sick and all. And then there was the possibility that you'd fire both of us."

"I wouldn't have done that," he stated firmly.

"Are you sure?"

He knew if he were honest he couldn't say yes. "I was a junior executive back then, eager to make my mark in the world. Maybe I was quick to rush to judgment, but at the time I had little choice. I, too, was under a lot of pressure.''

The rest of the journey was made in silence. As Jake parked outside her apartment, he turned to face her and was once more a bit taken aback by how lovely she looked this evening. Several curls had come loose from her chignon. He wanted to wrap them around his finger, gaze into her eyes and...

''It's late. I better go inside,'' she said, turning away from him to reach for the door handle.

''Wait,'' he commanded her. When she turned back to him, he said, ''I want to thank you for coming with me this evening.''

''You don't need to thank me. I only did what any good administrative assistant would have done,'' she told him.

Those words were like a splash of cold water on his face, reminding him of something he had been tempted to forget. That she was his employee and off-limits when it came to his personal feelings.

''I don't think dancing is in any administrative assistant's job description,'' he said dryly.

''I'm surprised I remember how. I don't get to do it very often,'' she remarked. ''It was nice.''

''You enjoyed it?''

''Couldn't you tell?''

''Actually, I could, which is why I felt a bit guilty. As we were swaying to the music, I thought that if you were my girl, I wouldn't want you out dancing with another man...even if he was your boss. I hope I haven't caused problems for you with your boyfriend.''

She gave him a puzzled look. ''How could you? I don't have a boyfriend.''

"You don't?" He remembered the scene in the jewelry store.

"No."

"Then you recently broke up with someone?"

She chuckled. "No, I'm afraid I don't have much time for a social life what with helping take care of Emma and my long hours at Temporarily Yours. Even though I'm single, I have family obligations."

Jake frowned. He didn't understand it. He had given her an opportunity to tell him about the man in her life, yet she insisted the man in the red pickup didn't exist. Why couldn't she tell him the truth?

She'd been awfully sexy on the dance floor, melting into him like butter into toast. She'd been more fun and more intriguing than the last dozen dates he'd had. And she had flirted with him and responded to him as a woman responds to a man she's interested in. Her behavior had not been that of someone with a steady boyfriend. He had given her the opportunity to admit that there was some other guy in her life, yet she hadn't.

Obviously, she didn't know that he had seen her shopping for rings with him and then watched as the guy had driven her to work the following morning. For all he knew, this guy could be sharing her apartment with her. Maybe that's why she'd insisted that he not come up when he came to get her earlier that evening.

It angered him that she could flirt with him when she was involved with another man. From the moment he picked her up, there had been a sparkle in her eyes he hadn't seen before. When they danced, it was as if an electric current moved from her body to his, creating a magical aura about them as they moved in rhythm to the music. He had had to use every ounce of willpower he possessed to resist the temptation to take her to a dark corner where they could be alone. His lips longed to kiss hers, to nuzzle the soft flesh he knew would be as sweet as the summery scent she wore.

"Well, good night," she said, unaware of the thoughts running through his head.

"I'll walk you to your door," he said stiffly.

"You don't have to. I'll be fine."

"I'm responsible for you this evening and I'd rather not have you being assaulted on my conscience," he said irritably, wondering if she was worried that he'd catch a glimpse of the blond fellow.

"How noble of you," Marcie muttered. "This might not be the most elite neighborhood in town, but it's not any more dangerous than any other area at night."

"Which is why I'm walking you to your door," he insisted, climbing out of the car. Despite her protest that he didn't need to come past the secured lobby door, he was determined to see just who shared her apartment.

When they reached the second floor, she stopped in front of a door with the number 212 on it and said, "You may leave now. I'm home safe and sound."

Jake was about to ask if he might come in for a cup of coffee when the door flew open and the man he'd seen in the jewelry store stood in the doorway.

"Marcie! We thought you'd never get home!"

Jake folded his arms over his chest, wondering how she was going to explain this *family obligation*.

"Tim, I'd like you to meet my employer, Jake Campbell. Jake, Tim is my—"

Before she could finish her sentence, however, a woman wandered to the door, barefoot and sleepy.

"Hi, come in! We waited for you so we could have dessert together. I made the most divine lemon pie."

"It's late, Peggy. I'm sure Mr. Campbell would like to get home."

Peggy's eyes brightened as she said, "Oh, so you're Marcie's boss."

Fascinated by the scenario that greeted him, Jake said, "Yes, and a piece of pie would be nice, thank you."

He followed Marcie's stiff-backed form into the room. She was uncomfortable, but he didn't care. If she was going to lie about her relationship with this man, then she deserved to feel uneasy.

As Jake entered the living room, he noticed that, although it was small, it had a certain charm. It was also filled with toys.

Marcie's sister put her hand on his arm. "May I take your coat? And please excuse the mess. I kept Emma up late to see her aunt Marcie, but she finally crashed about an hour ago. We had the whole arsenal of toys out as you can see. I realize there are enough in here for quintuplets, but that's Marcie's fault. She can't resist buying for Emma."

Her comments made Jake think of the day he and Marcie had shopped at the toy store in Chicago. When her eyes met his, he knew she was recalling the same thing.

"I suppose Marcie told you our big news," Peggy continued.

"News?" Jake looked curiously at the two sisters.

Peggy moved closer to the man named Tim, sliding her arm around his waist. "We're getting married." Shyly, Peggy held out her left hand to show off the ring. "Tim picked it out—with Marcie's help. Isn't that sweet? Pretty soon Emma will have a real daddy!'' Peggy hugged Tim's middle and he embraced her.

Jake offered his congratulations, giving Marcie an even wider grin than the one he gave the newly engaged couple. So Tim wasn't her boyfriend after all, but her future brother-in-law.

"You helped pick out the ring," Jake said as Marcie led him to a chair at the kitchen table.

"Yes. It's the reason I was late that Saturday morning we discovered the Farrell mistake. Peggy and Tim got a little carried away with the celebrating," she said in a low voice meant only for his ears. "I couldn't leave Emma until she came home."

"So Tim brought you to work." The puzzle pieces were falling into place.

"Yes. He's a sweetie. He's been so good for my sister, a real blessing."

Jake couldn't stop grinning. Marcie wasn't a liar. She didn't have a boyfriend. She was single and available.

He enjoyed the piece of pie and listening to Peggy tell tales about her sister, staying much later than he intended. As he left, he thought that this was a family he could enjoy being around.

Then he realized where his thoughts were taking him. Gradually, Marcie had been creeping into his thoughts, getting under his skin, and all the time he had forgotten something very important.

He was her boss and she was his subordinate. The first rule every employee agreed to adhere to when he or she signed on with his firm was not to mix business with pleasure. Office romance was forbidden. And he was a man who always followed the rules.

CHAPTER SEVEN

"WHAT'S wrong? Are you ill?" Jake asked Marcie when he returned from lunch the following Monday afternoon and saw her slumped over her desk.

She immediately straightened and tried to act as if nothing was out of the ordinary. "No, I'm fine. I was resting. That's all." Her cheeks were stained with color, which at first he thought was due to embarrassment at having been caught napping. But then he saw that she hadn't eaten her lunch. She had taken only a bite of the sandwich and the apple sat untouched.

"You didn't eat."

"I wasn't hungry," she told him. She wrapped the sandwich and shoved it back into the brown bag. "I'll save this for my break." She carried it over to the kitchenette where she returned it to the refrigerator. She looked tired, moving slowly as she walked back to her desk.

"You've been working above and beyond the call of duty. You don't need to stay late every night."

"It's all right. I'm used to working long hours," she told him with a smile he knew was falsely bright.

"You sure you're all right?"

"Yeah, I'm fine."

Next to the phone was a bottle from the pharmacy that she discreetly palmed and slid into her pocket. He didn't miss the gesture.

"I have the quarterly reports you wanted," she told him, reaching for a manila folder.

"Good. I'll need you to make some notes for me."

"Now?"

He guessed that she probably wanted to freshen up a bit. "Give me ten minutes and I'll be ready to go over them," he told her, then headed for his office.

Exactly ten minutes later she came into his office, looking much the same as she had when she had first woken from her nap. Most of the errant curls that had come loose from her chignon had been tucked back into place, but one stubborn coil refused to be tamed and dangled near her cheek in a most tantalizing way. She carried a glass of ice water in one hand, the manila folder in the other.

She set it on his desk and sat down in the leather chair across from him. She had removed her suit jacket so that the only thing covering her torso was a thin white blouse that made him want to forget about work. It softly draped her curves and gave her a very feminine look, reminding him that she was all woman beneath the businesslike persona she projected.

When she reached into her pocket for a throat lozenge, he said, "Are you sure you're feeling all right?"

"My throat's a little dry, but otherwise I'm fine." She unwrapped a lozenge and popped it into her mouth.

As they worked side by side, she gave him no reason to believe it was anything else, tackling the job with her usual tenacity. By the time they had finished with the reports, the glass of water was empty and several lozenge wrappers lay in the wastebasket.

"That'll do it for today. Don't forget that I'm going out of town this evening and will be back the day after tomorrow," he said as she gathered her things.

"What about your meeting with the Anderson brothers?"

"Reschedule for one day next week, will you?"

She looked as if she wanted nothing more than to go to bed, but she continued going over his scheduled appointments. Jake had a hunch that though she was trying hard to pretend nothing was wrong, she felt lousy.

Later that afternoon when he accidentally knocked a sheaf of papers off her desk, he discovered he was right. As they both stooped to retrieve them, his hand brushed hers. Her skin was hot to his touch.

"You're warm."

She didn't respond to his statement but gathered the scattered papers, saying, "I shouldn't have had these so close to the edge."

When she'd collected the papers and was about to walk back around the desk, he stopped her with a hand on her arm. Then he pressed his fingers to her forehead. "I'm no doctor, but it feels to me like you have a fever. That's why your cheeks are flushed and your throat is sore, isn't it?"

She nodded miserably, then sank onto her chair, holding her head in her hands. "I can't believe this is happening. I never get sick."

"Take the rest of the day off and go home," Jake ordered.

"I can't."

"Of course you can. If you're worried about the money, I'll pay you a full day's wages. Now pack up your things and get out of here. And if you're sick tomorrow, stay home."

She looked up at him with disbelief in her eyes. "You'll pay me even if I'm not here?"

"Yes. Brenda gets sick time."

"But I'm a temp. We only get paid for the hours we work."

"Are you arguing with the boss?"

"No, it's just that..." She hesitated, avoiding his eyes.

"It's just what?" he probed. "You're sick, Marcie. You should be home in bed."

"But that's the problem," she said as she once more bowed her head onto her hands. "I can't go home."

"Of course you can go home," he said, coming around the desk to stoop beside her. "I'm not an ogre. I won't have Sandra fire you for being ill."

"Thank you. I appreciate that, but I'd rather stay here until this evening...if that's all right with you."

She wasn't making any sense. He wondered if the fever was making her a bit delirious. "Why would you want to stay here when you're not feeling well?"

"Because the doctor said I'm contagious for the next twenty-four hours."

"You went to the doctor?"

She nodded. "On my lunch hour. "I have strep throat."

"Then you definitely should be home in bed." He put a hand on her arm and urged her to her feet.

"No, I can't go home just yet. If I do, Emma may get sick. She just got over a very bad bout of ear infections and the doctor says her immunity is low. What she doesn't need is to be exposed to this infection."

He could see why she was so upset. She was worried about her niece contracting the illness. He raked a hand across the back of his neck and sighed. "I can't let you stay here, Marcie."

"I won't be in anyone's way...I promise," she said with feverish, woeful eyes.

He walked over to the closet and retrieved her coat. "I have a better solution. You can spend the night at my place." He held her coat open so she could slip her arms in the sleeves.

"B-but I can't stay with you," she stammered. "You're my boss."

"You won't be staying *with* me. I'm going to New York tonight, remember?" He forced her arms into the coat sleeves. "You'll have the place to yourself. I'll call ahead and notify my housekeeper of the change of plan." He picked up the phone on Marcie's desk and made the call. As soon as he was done, he said to Marcie, "She'll stay until you get there. I told her to make you something to eat…some chicken soup or whatever it is that's good for bad throats."

"I'd rather stay here," she said, her voice breaking. "I should start feeling better shortly. I've already started the antibiotics."

"Don't be silly about this. Accept my offer. Peace and quiet, a warm meal and no risk of infecting your niece. And this way, if you're not feeling better in the morning, you'll have a place to stay."

He could see that she was too weak to argue. "All right. Thank you." She pulled her purse out from the desk drawer. "Can I take the bus?"

He guessed that, financially, it was the only mode of transportation she could afford. "I'll take you there myself."

"But you have to go to the airport."

"I have enough time," he assured her. "Ready?"

She nodded, then stopped in midstride on their way to the elevator. "Hold on. I should bring home those reports on the—"

He interrupted her before she could finish, taking her by the arm. "The reports can wait."

For once she didn't argue with him.

Marcie had suspected since the first day she walked into the firm that its chief executive officer made more money in one year than she would probably ever see in her lifetime. That's why it came as no surprise to her that he would live in an exclusive residential area populated with homes that looked more like estates pictured in the back of some classy magazine.

"I'm not going to be a prisoner here, am I?" she asked after a security guard in a small building nodded at Jake and opened the wrought-iron gates that allowed them access to the neighborhood.

"He keeps people out, not residents in," he answered.

Marcie wasn't so sure. Ever since Jake had helped her on with her coat, she felt as if he had taken control of her life, making decisions for her, treating her as if he was responsible for her. She did feel a bit like his prisoner, being swept off to his castle where she had no way of escaping without his permission.

As he drove down wooded lanes past huge houses Marcie could only describe as mansions, she realized that even if she wanted to get away, she wouldn't be able to. There was no city bus this far from town and it would cost a small fortune to take a cab.

"How do I get to work tomorrow?" she asked.

"I'll arrange to have a car pick you up...if you're feeling well enough to go in."

"Of course I'll be well enough. I'm on antibiotics."

"You can make that decision in the morning. Clara will take good care of you no matter what."

"She's your housekeeper?"

"Yes. She's nursed me through many illnesses. She was my nanny when I was a child."

That made Marcie wonder what kind of child he must have been. He was always so serious, she wondered if he had ever really been a kid. Had he ever laughed and played at the park or had he always been intent upon adultlike things? According to what she'd heard at the award dinner, he'd started his own business when he was ten. A junior achiever, they'd called him.

One thing for certain was that he definitely had a penchant for making money, and once Marcie saw his home she knew that he had plenty. Stone pillars marked the entrance of the paved horseshoe drive in front of the two-story brick residence. Although it was only early April and the grass was still dormant, splashes of color lined the walk as daffodils and tulips bloomed in abundance.

"Since I'll be leaving shortly, I'll park out front," he told her as he brought the car to a stop in front of the columned entrance. He came around to her side of the car, where he opened her door and helped her out.

When he didn't release her arm as he ushered her toward the front door, she said, "I'm all right."

"You look like you're about ready to keel over," he answered.

She was, but not because of the fever. The thought of spending the night in his house was a daunting one. Now that she was on the doorstep, she had a crazy urge to run back to the car and order him to take her anywhere but here.

She didn't. She swallowed back the fear that threatened to make her knees knock and allowed him to lead her inside.

The minute they stepped into the tiled foyer, a short woman wearing a black dress with a white apron greeted them. "You must be Marcie. How are you feeling?" She hovered close as Marcie unbuttoned her coat.

"Marcie, meet Clara," Jake said as he helped her out of her coat.

"Let me take that." Clara tried to take the garment from Jake's hands, but he wouldn't let her.

"I'll put this away. You take Marcie upstairs to her room."

Clara looked at Marcie and asked, "Do you need to lie down or would you like me to make you something to eat?"

"Oh, I don't think I could eat anything," Marcie answered.

The older woman placed her hand on Marcie's forehead. "It's no wonder you feel so awful. You're burning up."

Marcie took a step back. "You shouldn't get so close. I'm contagious."

Clara simply blew a burst of air through her lips and said, "You're not giving me anything I don't come into contact with every day."

Seeing Marcie's puzzled look, Jake explained, "Clara volunteers every morning at the local school. Helps kids with their reading."

"But this is nasty stuff," Marcie reminded him.

Clara waved her hand. "Not to worry. If I haven't caught it by now, I'm not going to get it." She put a slightly gnarled hand beneath Marcie's and urged her down the hallway. "Jake will tell you I make not only the tastiest but the most therapeutic soup in the state of Minnesota.''

Marcie looked at Jake helplessly.

''It's true. If Clara's soup doesn't make you feel better, nothing will.''

She could see that she was going to get no help from him. ''I...'' she began, then gave up. The way she was feeling at the moment it was probably best just to let someone else make decisions for her.

So into the kitchen she went, trying not to look awed by the splendor of Jake's home. But she was overwhelmed. Having humble roots, Marcie had spent most of her life living in apartments that had only enough space for the barest of necessities. She couldn't help it if her mouth dropped open not only at the size of the house but also the elegant furnishings surrounding her.

For years she had prepared meals on a narrow strip of countertop in an efficiency apartment. Seeing the amount of space Clara had for work brought a sigh of envy to Marcie's lips. Besides several rows of cabinets and an island with an additional cooktop and sink, the kitchen had every convenience a cook could want.

Clara led her to a large wooden table and pulled out one of the chairs for her. ''You sit here and it'll only take me a couple of minutes to get you that soup.'' She patted her hand in a maternal way that reminded Marcie of her own mother's touch.

''Thank you,'' she said, swallowing back the emotion the memory triggered.

When Jake sat down next to her, Clara said, ''Aren't you supposed to be at the airport?''

''I won't miss my plane,'' he assured her. Then he gave her a wonderful smile as he said, ''You ought to know by now I'm never late.''

That smile did funny things to Marcie's equilibrium—or was it the fever? She didn't think she wanted to know the answer.

"Clara, where's the thermometer? I think we should take Marcie's temperature," he said.

"There's one in the medicine cabinet in the main bath," Clara answered as she stood in front of the stove with a wooden spoon in hand.

As Jake went to leave, Marcie stopped him. "No, you don't have to get it. I'm fine. Really."

He ignored her, walking away and disappearing down the hallway.

"How about a cup of tea? Or maybe you'd prefer juice?" Clara asked as she set a linen napkin and silver in front of Marcie.

"Tea would be nice," she answered, thinking that it would be good to have something soothing on her throat.

Clara continued to fuss, setting honey, cream and sugar on the table. By the time Jake returned, the teakettle was whistling and the soup was warm.

"I couldn't find it," he said on a note of frustration.

"It doesn't matter," Marcie assured him. "I'm on the antibiotics."

"Is it time for you to take them?" he asked.

Marcie was surprised by Jake's attentiveness. She would never have expected him to fuss over anyone who was sick and especially not when that someone was her. Silently, she opened her purse and pulled out the prescription bottle, shaking a tablet into her hand.

"She needs water," Jake said to Clara.

"It's all right. I can take it with my tea," Marcie told them both, wishing they would stop treating her as if she were one step from needing a hospital bed.

She felt like a bug under a magnifying glass with the two of them watching every move she made. She wished Jake would leave for the airport. Clara's attention she appreciated. His was another story.

Seeing him at ease in his own home made their relationship seem less professional and more personal—which was ridiculous. Just because she was sitting in his kitchen eating chicken soup didn't mean he was no longer her boss.

The more solicitous he became toward her, the more tempting it was to regard him as something other than her temporary employer. And what she didn't need was more thoughts along those lines. She'd been having enough of them already. That's why she was relieved when he finally stood and announced that he was leaving for the airport.

"You better take care," Clara warned him. "They say there might be some fog this evening."

Jake kissed his housekeeper on the cheek and assured her that he'd be very careful. Then he turned to Marcie and said, "Remember what I said. If you're not feeling better in the morning, stay in bed. Clara's got the number for the taxi if you need it."

She nodded weakly and thanked him again for his generosity. He brushed aside her gratitude by saying she wouldn't be of any use to him in the office if she let her condition worsen.

After he was gone, Clara continued to fuss over her, but she discovered the attention was a comfort. The older woman was a kind, gentle soul who reminded Marcie so much of her mother that she found herself telling her more about herself than she intended. They quickly became friends, and as soon as Marcie had finished the soup, Clara hustled her up the stairs to an opulent guest room that made the ritzy hotel she and Jake had stayed at in Chicago pale in comparison.

Thick, plush carpet cushioned her feet as she walked over to a bed covered with an old-fashioned puffed comforter that was a patchwork of pale blues and white. Dozens of pillows trimmed with eyelet lace graced the four-poster bed.

All the furniture in the room had a dark cherry finish, including the huge armoire, which Clara soon pointed out was actually an entertainment center. With the touch of a remote she could watch television, listen to the stereo or play a videotape. There was also a writing desk, a vanity and a chest of drawers.

"This room is lovely," she told Clara, setting her purse down on the small round table beside the bed. It was draped in the same blue-and-white fabric that graced the windows and the bed.

"There's a full bath in here," the older woman stated, pushing open a door on the other side of the armoire. "I've set fresh towels out for you and there are bath crystals or scented shower gel if you prefer."

"Thank you, but I wish you hadn't gone to so much trouble."

"It's no trouble whatsoever. Makes me feel as if I'm earning that enormous salary Jake pays me. He's such a dear boy," she cooed affectionately.

Dear boy? Marcie knew her boss was no boy. He was a very handsome, virile man who could be tender when he wanted to be. The way he treated Clara was proof of that.

As the housekeeper turned down the bed and fluffed the pillows, she said, "Except for the times when his family comes to visit, we seldom have guests, which is really a shame. This is a grand house for entertaining," she said with a smile.

Marcie wondered why Jake didn't often have company stay with him. It did seem a shame to have a house this big and no one to share it with.

"You're looking rather pale, dear." Clara gave Marcie's shoulder a gentle squeeze. "I need to quit blabbering away and let you get to sleep."

"No, it's all right. I enjoy talking with you, Clara."

"There'll be plenty of time for that in the morning. What time should I be here for your breakfast?"

Not accustomed to having someone wait on her, Marcie said, "Oh, please don't come just because of me. If Jake's going to be out of town and you're supposed to have the day off, you don't need to come in for me."

"I did have plans to go down to Winona to see my cousin...." The housekeeper looked very uncertain.

"Then by all means go. Please. You'll make me feel awful if I think I've kept you from enjoying your day off. And by morning I'm sure I'll be feeling a lot better and I am perfectly capable of making myself some toast."

"If you're sure..."

"Yes. Take your day off. I'll be fine."

"All right, but only if you promise you'll call me if you're not feeling better."

"I promise," Marcie said, holding up her hand in oathlike fashion.

"Good. If you think of anything you might need, you can call me. I'm number one on the speed dial," she said, gesturing to the phone on the small round table.

Then she picked up a starched white dress shirt that

had been draped over the back of a padded blue chair. "When Jake said you didn't have a change of clothes with you, I figured you'd need something to sleep in. You can use this." Seeing Marcie's hesitance to take the shirt from her, she added, "Now don't go worrying that it's one of his good shirts. It's not. You can see the cuffs are getting a little frayed around the edges."

It wasn't the age of the shirt that made Marcie reluctant to borrow it. How could she sleep in something that had been worn by Jake?

"Are you sure he won't mind?" she finally asked.

Clara flapped her hand, dismissing the question as trivial. "He has so many shirts he won't even realize one is missing."

That did little to ease Marcie's mind. Whether or not Jake wanted her to use the shirt wasn't really the issue. It was the thought of wearing something so personal of his that bothered Marcie. Here she was in his house, eating his food, wearing his clothing...

"You'd better take it. If you need to get up in the night, you'll want something to protect you from the chill. It's that time of the year. No matter how high I set the thermostat, the house still feels drafty."

Marcie knew she had a point. She supposed she could have slept in her slip and underwear, but if she used Jake's shirt she could hand wash her lingerie and have it clean the next day.

"Thank you. I will use it," she told Clara, taking the shirt from her outstretched hand.

"Good. Now, if you want to walk me down to the front door, I'll show you how to set the security alarm. You'll need to do that when you leave in the morning, too." Marcie nodded and followed her down the spiral staircase to the door where Clara gave her instructions for setting the electronic security system before putting on her coat to leave. "It's been a real pleasure meeting you, Marcie," she said with a sincerity that touched Marcie's heart. "I feel as if we could easily become friends."

"I feel the same way about you, Clara. Jake is lucky to have you."

Catching Marcie off guard, the older woman pulled her into her arms and gave her a bear hug. "I know you're sick, but I couldn't resist," she said before Marcie could protest. "You have a good night's rest now and make sure you call if you need me, okay?"

Marcie agreed and waved goodbye, then punched in the code that activated the security system as soon as the heavy wood door was shut. Suddenly, without Clara's presence, the house felt strange and impersonal. She hurried up the stairs and back to the guest room where she wasted no time in getting ready for bed.

The house did have a chill to it, she discovered as she undressed, and she was grateful Clara had left her the white dress shirt. In the bathroom she found a brand-new toothbrush and assorted toiletries for her use. As Marcie stared into the mirror, she could see why Jake and Clara had been so concerned. Her skin was a sickly shade of gray and there were dark circles beneath her eyes.

She hadn't realized just how badly her body ached until she slid into bed between the smooth sheets. It was a most comfortable mattress, and even though she was in a strange house, it felt so good just to be able to lie down she didn't care whose house it was. She set the alarm on the clock beside the bed and snuggled down into the covers.

As she drifted off to sleep, her thoughts were of Jake.

She had seen a side to him tonight that she could get used to seeing on a regular basis.

That was a dangerous thought. Once her stint as his temp was over, she'd never see him again. But she couldn't think about that. She was tired. And she *would* see him again in two days. In the office. Where he would be his usual stern self.

She sighed and fell asleep.

CHAPTER EIGHT

MARCIE wasn't sure what it was that woke her, but she immediately sensed she was in unfamiliar surroundings. The pillowy-soft comforter told her she wasn't in her own bed. She blinked, then looked at the clock on the table beside the bed. It was after midnight and she was at Jake's.

Feeling thirsty, she thought she'd get a glass of water and switched on the lamp. When her stomach twinged with hunger, she decided instead to go downstairs and pour herself a glass of milk as well as fill a pitcher with water. She climbed out of bed and padded across the soft carpet. As she opened her bedroom door, she saw that the light was on in the entry. She traced several fingers across her forehead, trying to remember if she had turned it off before climbing the stairs. Obviously she hadn't, which she could only blame on her eagerness to get to bed.

Carefully, she padded down the hallway toward the staircase. Wearing only the white dress shirt, she moved quickly, shivering as she made her way to the first floor. Before heading for the kitchen, she double-checked the alarm and breathed a bit more easily when the indicator light told her the security system was activated and working properly.

The tiled foyer was cold beneath her feet as she scurried toward the kitchen. To her surprise, the light was also on in that room. Marcie frowned. Surely Clara had turned everything off before she left? Marcie hadn't taken but two steps into the kitchen when she heard a voice behind her.

"Where are you going?"

She let out a shriek. "What are you doing here?"

"I live here," Jake said, amusement dancing in his eyes.

"But...but...you're supposed to be in New York," she stammered, her heart still racing from fright.

"I couldn't go. The airport was fogged in. All flights were canceled."

"You scared me," she scolded him, pressing a hand against her heart.

"I'm sorry."

"No, you're not!" She could see that he was doing his best to hold back a smile. "You think it's funny!" she accused. "You could have called and told me you were coming back home."

"I didn't want to wake you. I thought you'd be in bed sleeping," he said in an annoyingly calm voice, the grin still trying to break loose.

"I was, but I got thirsty." She was suddenly aware that she was wearing nothing but an extra large man's shirt. From the way Jake was staring at her, the fact hadn't escaped his attention. His eyes gleamed with an almost predatory look as he studied her. "I have to fill this," she said, grabbing a pitcher and thrusting it out in front of her.

He took it from her hands. "I'll do it."

She didn't protest. It would be wiser to have his thoughts and hands occupied than to have him watching her fumble with the container. He walked over to the refrigerator and pulled out a large bottle of water.

"You don't have to give me designer water. I drink it straight from the tap when I'm at home."

"Well, you're not at home, are you?" he said as he unscrewed the cap and emptied the contents of the bottle into the pitcher. "This water is better for you. No contaminants. It's what a person who is ill should be drinking. How are you feeling, by the way?"

"Better. I think the fever's gone, but my throat's still a little scratchy," she told him, wishing she didn't feel as if she were half-naked.

A glance down at her bare legs told her there was a reason she felt so exposed. She was. The shirt allowed him a glimpse of leg he normally wouldn't see. She supposed she could be glad that she was at least wearing his shirt. If she had slept in her lingerie, she'd be standing before him in lacy underwear. Judging by the look on his face, she thought it probably was a toss-up as to which would be the more provocative.

She wished she knew how to handle herself in such a situation. She was twenty-four years old, but except for one somewhat steady boyfriend in college, she had had very little experience with men. A social life had never been a priority. With her mother dying when she was only nineteen, there had never been any time for Marcie to have a relationship with a man. All her energy had gone into seeing that she and Peggy had a roof over their heads and food on the table.

Maybe some women could have smoothed over the awkwardness of being caught in her situation with a smile and a few well-chosen words, but Marcie felt incapable of any coherent conversation at this point. Especially not when Jake was looking at her as if she were a giant cream puff he wanted to eat.

"Clara took good care of you?" he asked, one eye on the water pouring out of the bottle, the other on her.

"Yes. She's sweet. You're lucky to have her."

"Yes, I am."

They continued to make small talk while Jake filled the pitcher. He had thought that after her initial shock at his appearance, she would relax, but she continued to fidget nervously. When she slid around to the opposite side of the island counter, he was quite certain it was an attempt at modesty. Not that hiding those lovely legs could diminish the sexual tension between them at the moment. The air practically crackled with it.

And with good reason. Tousled from sleep and wearing nothing but his shirt, she had never looked more charming. It wasn't her bare legs that held his attention, but her hair. It fell in glorious disarray around her shoulders. Big, gold, bouncing curls that begged for his fingers to wrap themselves around them.

"Is there anything else I can get you? A snack maybe?" he asked, reluctant to send her back to the guest room.

"No, I don't think a snack would be a good idea," she answered.

"Stomach a bit uneasy?"

"Not exactly," she hedged.

When her stomach growled, he grinned. "You *are* hungry. Let me get you something to eat."

"No, I don't think so," she said, shifting from one foot to the other.

"There's plenty of food in the refrigerator." He opened the door to show her.

"I know, but—"

"But what?"

She hesitated before speaking, as if carefully choosing her words. "You're my boss and I'm standing in your kitchen in the middle of the night wearing—" she looked down at the dress shirt "—this."

"Yes, and I must say it looks much better on you than it ever did on me." So good, it was causing him to consider throwing caution to the wind and forget that she was his employee. For weeks he had been fighting his attraction to her, telling himself that she was not the sort of woman he would want in his private life. Now he knew that just the opposite was true.

"If Sandra found out, she would have reason to fire me," Marcie said weakly.

"I wouldn't let her do that," he assured her, unable to resist reaching across the counter to stroke her pale cheek. She trembled at his touch.

"You shouldn't," she said in a voice that was barely a whisper.

"Why not?" he whispered back, loving the velvety smoothness of her skin.

"You know why."

The message in her eyes contradicted the words she spoke. Fortunately, for both of them, the heat of her flesh reminded him that there was more than one reason he shouldn't be touching her. Reluctantly, he removed his fingers from her cheek. "You feel as if you still might have a bit of a fever. You should be in bed."

She nodded.

"Are you spending the night here?"

"Yes. I told you my flight was canceled."

"Then I can't stay." She stepped back, folding her arms across her chest. "Thank you for everything you've done," she went on in a rush, "but I'm really feeling much better now and I'm sure that I'll be just fine once I get dressed and—"

"What are you talking about? You're not going anywhere at this time of night. Take your water and go back upstairs to bed," he ordered. "Your boss has spoken."

She chewed on her lower lip as she considered his command.

"Think of this as a business trip—just like our trip to Chicago," he pointed out. "Only instead of sharing a suite, we have this big house."

She lowered her eyes. "You must think I'm foolish."

"No, I think you're a very conscientious employee and I'm lucky to have you. Tonight is not the time, but someday, when you're not a guest in my home, we need to talk."

"You mean about my job?" she asked weakly, risking a glance at him.

"No, I mean about us."

"All right," she said quietly. "I'll go upstairs now. Thank you for the water."

With a casual good-night tossed over her shoulder, she hurried across the kitchen tiles. Before she could disappear from the room, however, he called out to her, causing her to stop and turn around.

"One more thing. There's no point in my taking a flight to New York tomorrow since I can't possibly get there in time for my appointment. I'll be going into the office instead. I'll give you a ride if you feel well enough to go in."

"I will be," she said confidently. "I'll have to go home and change clothes first, of course."

"That's not a problem. I plan to leave by seven."

She nodded. "Clara's not going to be here to cook breakfast, but I could fix you something if you like."

He rejected her offer. "That's not necessary. As

Clara would tell you, I seldom eat breakfast. I only grab a cup of coffee, which I take with me in the car."

She smiled then, a funny little wistful grin. "Better not let your mother hear you say that."

He grinned, too. "No, she already thinks I'm a workaholic who seldom stops to eat."

"You do eat quite a few lunches at your desk."

"You know me well." Again the room filled with a tension that had nothing to do with work.

Without another word, she was gone. Jake gave her time to climb the stairs before retiring to his own room, hoping if she was out of sight, she'd be out of mind.

Unfortunately, he had to lie awake a long time before that happened. For no matter how hard he tried to focus on work, all he could see when he closed his eyes were those gorgeous blond curls framing a lovely face.

Just as Jake expected, Marcie was dressed and ready to go the following morning. When he stepped into the kitchen, he found her sitting at the island counter on a tall stool eating cantaloupe.

"Oh, is it that time?" She started to hop down from the stool, but he stopped her.

"Finish your breakfast. I can wait."

She got down off the stool anyway. "You need your coffee."

"I can get it."

She paid no attention but scurried around him, fixing it just the way he liked—with milk and sugar. "Clara left some lemon poppy-seed muffins if you want me to get you one."

"No, coffee's all I need," he assured her.

She climbed back on the stool and dug into her fresh

fruit. "Clara's a dear. I told her I could get my own breakfast, but she insisted on cutting up this cantaloupe for me," she said, using her spoon to point to the cubed melon in her bowl.

"You must be feeling better. Your appetite's back," he said, watching her devour a muffin as well as the fruit.

"Yes. The sore throat's gone and so is my headache. The doctor was right. The antibiotic kicked in just as he predicted."

"You're sure you feel up to working?"

"Yes, I am." She washed down a bite of muffin with a sip of tea and said, "I'm ready when you are." With the same efficiency with which she ran his office, she tidied up the kitchen, saying, "You're going to be on your own for dinner. Clara thought you were going to be gone until tomorrow and went down to Winona to see her cousin."

"I think I can manage to feed myself."

With one last check to make sure everything was in order, Marcie steered him out the door. Gone was any trace of the woman who had stood in his kitchen last night dressed in one of his shirts.

At that memory, his body responded in a typically male way. It had taken every bit of his willpower not to pull her into his arms and kiss her senseless last night. Seeing those shapely legs and the gentle curves barely hidden by the white cotton had made his imagination run wild. He wished that she had been in his room making love instead of staying in a guest bedroom because she was sick.

"The light's green," Marcie said, interrupting his fantasies, and he realized that he had been daydreaming. He tried to focus his attention back on the road, but her presence alongside him was a distraction he couldn't ignore. "I want to thank you for letting me stay in your home last night," she added a moment later. "It was very kind of you."

He chuckled. "I think that's the first time you've ever called me kind. You still think I'm that big an ogre at work?"

He cast a sideways glance at her and noticed her cheeks had just a hint of red to them. "I never thought you were an ogre."

Again he chuckled. "I thought we'd agreed that honesty was the only way we were going to make our relationship work."

"Do we have a relationship?" she asked.

"Professional, yes. Personal…that's still up for discussion, isn't it?"

"It shouldn't be." She was looking down at her hands folded neatly in her lap. "Sandra O'Neill has strict rules about becoming personally involved with clients."

"And I'm sure you've been told by Human Resources that there are similar rules at the investment firm, as well."

"And your being the CEO…well, you must be an exemplary role model for the others, right?"

"Marcie, when I'm with you, I find myself wanting to break lots of rules."

He wasn't sure what he expected her response to be to this admission, but it wasn't the gasp she emitted as he whizzed right through an intersection on a green light.

"You missed the turn!"

He *had* missed the turn. If he didn't stop thinking about Marcie, he wasn't going to be of much use to anyone today. It was with relief that he dropped her off in front of her apartment complex. While she ran upstairs to change her clothes, he reached for the *Wall Street Journal*.

Not that reading did him any good. He thought how ironic it was that only a few weeks ago he had wanted to call Sandra O'Neill and demand that she remove Marcie from his office. Now he didn't want to think of a day without her.

Although the end of her stint as his temporary assistant wasn't far away. As much as he hated to see it coming, at least it meant that he could have another kind of relationship with her. Then neither one of them would need to worry about how they behaved with each other. After all, there were no rules about dating ex-employees.

But he didn't want to wait until she was no longer his assistant to take her out on a date. And he wouldn't. Rules or no rules. By the time she came bouncing down the steps of the apartment complex, he had made up his mind.

"Is everything okay?" he asked as he helped her into the car.

"Yes, Emma and Peggy are both healthy. No sign of any sore throats."

"Then it was good that you spent last night at my place," he said before closing the door. When he was once again seated behind the wheel, he asked, "Do you have plans for this evening?"

"Just the usual—help Peggy with Emma," she answered. "Why?"

"Because I'd like you to have dinner with me."

She shrugged. "I guess if they got along without me last night, they can get along without me tonight."

She didn't sound very excited at the prospect of having dinner with him. Disappointment hit him like a fist in the stomach, yet he wasn't a man to give up easily. "Then do we have a date?"

"A date?" she said on a squeak of surprise.

"Yes. As I told you last night, we need to talk. About us." He reached for her hand and brought her fingers to his lips. "I want there to be an us, Marcie. Don't you?"

She smiled then, a wonderful smile that made him feel as if he could do anything if he put his mind to it. "Yes, I want there to be an us, too, but what about the rules?"

"For once in my life, I'm going to ignore the rules." He brushed a curl back from her cheek.

"It could be dangerous," she said coyly, her eyes sparkling.

"I'm willing to take the risk if you are. So what do you say?"

"You're the boss."

Yes, he was, and he should have known better than to get involved with an employee. As he pulled away from the curb, there was one thought going round and round in his head. Was he playing with fire, and if so, would he get burned?

It had been a long time since Marcie had had a date. Too long, she decided, as jitters had her fumbling with the clasp on her necklace. It didn't help that the date was with her boss.

Her sister, however, saw no reason for Marcie to be nervous. After all, he was just a guy. Maybe to Peggy he was, but to Marcie he was someone who had captured her heart when she wasn't looking.

Which was why she was so nervous about their date. She wanted the evening to be special.

And it was. He took her to an exclusive restaurant high atop an office tower. Noted for its romantic setting, it provided patrons with the most breathtaking view of the city. Soft background music, candlelight and secluded tables made it the perfect destination for a quiet dinner for two.

Besides a strolling violinist, a young woman selling roses circulated among the guests. When she passed their table, Jake signaled for her to stop. From the variety of roses she carried, he chose one that was a deep shade of red and handed it to Marcie.

"Thank you. It's lovely," she said, sniffing the flower appreciatively.

"So are you."

She was grateful the lighting was dim so that he wouldn't see her blush. She glanced out the plate-glass window and said, "The city is spectacular at night, isn't it?"

"You like the view from up here?"

"Yes, it's wonderful." She rambled on about some of the landmarks she could identify, feeling extremely gauche but not knowing what else to say. Now that Jake was no longer her adversary, she found her self-confidence had evaporated.

She was grateful for the appearance of the waiter. At least while Jake ordered dinner, she didn't feel like his eyes were devouring her. The reprieve didn't last long, however, and as soon as they were once more alone, he fixed her with a penetrating gaze that sent both a wave of longing and a frisson of uneasiness through her.

"You know, you had me quite worried yesterday,"

he said, leaning closer to her. "You looked as if you might faint right there in the office."

"I felt awful." She reached for her glass and took a sip of water. As she set it back down, she clanged the stem against her plate, nearly spilling the contents.

He reached across the table for her hand. "You don't need to be nervous around me, Marcie."

"I'm not," she said, a wave of warmth rushing through her at his touch.

"Yes, you are. Ever since we arrived, you've been acting like a bird who's worried there's a cat on her tail." He gave her a devilishly attractive grin and added, "I'm not a cat."

She shifted uneasily. "Somehow, I feel as if we should be discussing work. What if someone were to see us out together?"

"And that's why you're nervous?"

"The last time I broke company rules I got fired. Remember?"

"That was different."

"Because I wasn't breaking the rules with you?" She immediately felt contrite. "I'm sorry. I shouldn't have said that. We've already agreed that the past should be the past."

"If I could go back, I'd change a few things," he admitted, much to her surprise.

"Me, too," she agreed. "I did make a lot of mistakes."

"Everyone does when they're young."

"So you think I've changed?"

"I know you have. These past weeks I've realized that the young girl who bungled her way through my office five years ago is gone. In her place is an experienced, intelligent woman who has done something no other woman has ever been able to do.''

''What's that?''

''Keep up with me. As efficient as Brenda is, she hasn't been able to do some of the things you've accomplished.''

He couldn't have said more potent words of praise. ''I appreciate your saying that. I've worked very hard to do the best job I could.''

''And you've done a wonderful job.''

''Is that why you brought me here tonight? To say thank-you?''

He gave her a look that made her stomach feel as if she'd gone down very fast in an elevator. ''I thought we'd already determined why I asked you out this evening.''

''You said it was a date.''

''Yes. I wanted to have dinner with a beautiful woman whose company I enjoy.''

She lowered her eyes, afraid he'd see what was in her heart. Having dinner together was one thing, but falling in love...that was an entirely different matter. And being with Jake tonight made her realize that that was exactly what had happened in the past month. She'd fallen in love with her boss.

Just then, the waiter returned with their appetizer. From that moment on, Jake didn't once mention business throughout the course of the meal. They discussed films and books and dozens of other topics, but not one word about the financial world.

For Marcie it was a magical night. Jake was charming and witty, and by the time he took her home she realized that the thought of having to get up and go to work the next day didn't fill her with anxiety, but excitement. For weeks she had been counting the days until she'd no longer have to be Jake's assistant. Now she didn't want to think about that time coming.

When he pulled up outside her apartment, he didn't get out of the car right away, but laid his arm across the back of her seat and said, "I'm sorry this evening must come to an end."

"Me, too," she said, her heart rate increasing at the thought that he was going to kiss her. "Thank you for dinner...and for the rose." She sniffed the flower that lay in her lap.

"Thank *you* for proving me wrong," he said close to her face.

Puzzled, she looked up at him. "Wrong about what?"

"Thinking that I couldn't trust you."

"And now you know you can?"

"You're not only trustworthy, you're creative, intelligent, honest, conscientious..."

She looked down at her hands. "Better watch out or I might ask for a raise," she said lightly, trying not to let him see just how much his words meant to her.

"I'm beginning to think you may be priceless."

Marcie's breath caught in her throat at the look in his eyes. He placed a finger under her chin and drew her closer to him, saying, "I know I'm not supposed to do this, but I can't resist."

Jake's lips closed over hers in the most wonderful kiss Marcie had ever experienced. His mouth moved sensuously over hers, coaxing her lips to open so he could caress her with his tongue. Every nerve in her body came alive, creating a tingling of pleasure that had her trembling as her body pressed against his.

As he pulled her closer, she could feel the beat of

his heart echoing the thundering rhythm of her own. One kiss became two and then three until finally she no longer knew when one kiss ended and another began. By the time he finally released her, they were both breathing raggedly. She felt the warmth of his breath as he rested his forehead against hers.

"I would like to do so much more than kiss you, but this isn't the time or the place," he said huskily. He straightened and ran a hand across his hair. "There are some rules we shouldn't bend. And even though when I'm with you I feel as though nothing in the world matters except us, the fact is you are still my employee."

"For a few more days anyway," she said, a bit dazed by his words.

"Yes." He planted one more kiss on her lips, then straightened, placing his hands on the steering wheel and gazing out at the street. "As much as I hate to say this, I'm going to have to treat you like my assistant for the remainder of those days."

"I understand."

"Do you?" He turned to meet her gaze, a plea in his eyes.

"Of course."

He opened his door and climbed out. Coming around to her side of the car, he was the perfect gentleman, escorting her up the steps and into the building. He walked her to her apartment, where she gave him the key and allowed him to unlock the door for her.

Before stepping inside, she said, "Thank you again. I had a wonderful time."

He bent his head and kissed her. What started as a light, tender kiss soon became a wild and hungry caress that had him reluctantly pulling away from her. "In a few days there'll be no reason for me not to kiss you like that. But tonight…'' He trailed off, his eyes telling her just how hard it was for him to stop.

''I'd better go inside.'' Her voice was as wobbly as her knees.

He nodded. ''But as you go to sleep tonight, remember this. In a few days we won't have to worry about rules.''

CHAPTER NINE

EVEN though it was a dismal day with rain pelting the office windows, Jake felt as if there wasn't a cloud in the sky. By this time next week Brenda would be back and he could begin a relationship with Marcie that would have nothing to do with the investment firm.

His feelings for her had developed so quickly he'd been caught off guard. Just the thought of her sitting in the outer office sent the blood rushing through his veins. As wonderful as she was as an assistant, he knew it was a good thing her temporary assignment was nearly over. His ability to concentrate on his work had been severely hampered since Marcie's arrival. Recently, he had had to force himself to think about investment strategies when what he really wanted to do was call her into his office and find out as much as he could about her.

Yes, it was definitely a good thing she was leaving at the end of the week. He could only imagine what his co-workers would say if they found out that he had been breaking one of the rules of conduct—no dating the staff.

It was the first time in his career that he had found the rule impossible to follow. Five years ago he had had no trouble at all keeping his relationship with Marcie from developing into anything personal. At the time he had been so intent upon establishing a reputation in the investment industry that he wouldn't have even considered breaking a rule to be with a woman.

He chuckled as he thought about it. When he was younger, everyone would have expected him to be a bit reckless when it came to love. Now he was older and supposedly wiser, yet here he was in a position of responsibility in which he should be setting an example and he was acting like some young love-struck kid.

His musings were interrupted by Marcie, who beeped him to say that Brenda was on line one. It didn't take long before his good mood disintegrated. He couldn't believe what he had heard. Brenda wasn't coming back. She had decided to start a whole new life with her husband—one that didn't include the stress of working in an investment firm that required its employees to put in such long hours.

Jake stared at the receiver for several seconds before finally putting it back on its cradle. Now what would he do? He raked a hand across his hair, then called Human Resources and learned that it would probably take at least a month to fill the permanent position.

Which meant Jake had no choice but to reach for the phone and call Sandra O'Neill.

"I'm going to need a temp for another month," he told her, then went on to explain about Brenda's resignation.

"Well, you're in luck. I had scheduled Marcie for another assignment, but just this morning I heard from that client that there had been a change in plans. Tell me the exact dates you need her."

He shifted uncomfortably in his chair. "I'd rather you send someone other than Marcie."

There was a brief silence on the other end and Jake could only imagine the surprise his request had created.

"I thought you were happy with her performance," Sandra finally responded.

"She's done a very good job," he confirmed.

"Then I don't understand. She's the most qualified person I have for that position...I've already told you that."

"Yes, I realize that, but I'd prefer another temp."

He didn't want to admit the reason why. He couldn't, not without the risk of getting Marcie in trouble. She had told him that Sandra O'Neill had the same type of policy at her agency. Professional relationships were to remain professional. There was no place for romance in the office.

"My request is no reflection upon Ms. MacLean's performance," he assured her. "She's represented your agency well and will receive the bonus we agreed upon."

"That's a relief to hear," Sandra said on a sigh.

"I expect you'll be able to send me another competent temp in her place."

"I'll do my best to find you a replacement for Marcie, Jake, but it won't be easy. I'll have to call you back after I've made some inquiries."

"Very well." They exchanged a few pleasantries, then ended the conversation.

Jake hated to make such a request. Marcie was an excellent assistant and he knew she'd continue to make his work easier for him if she stayed another four weeks. The problem was he didn't want her working for him.

He wanted to be able to take her to dinner and not discuss business. He wanted to take her dancing and not worry that he was holding her too close. He wanted to kiss her and not be concerned that someone from the office might see them and report back that he, the CEO, was breaking his own rule. He wanted to put romance into her life—something he couldn't do if she continued to be a member of his staff.

As tempting as it had been to tell Sandra he wanted Marcie to continue working with him, he was glad he didn't do it. Next week, while he suffered through the woes of breaking in a new temp, he'd remind himself that at least in the evening he'd see Marcie. Talk to her, take her to dinner...hold her in his arms.

In just a few days they could officially become a couple. They'd celebrate their new beginning with the perfect date on Saturday. Several of his colleagues were getting together for the golden wedding anniversary of one of the firm's biggest clients. The private dining room of an exclusive hotel had been reserved for the occasion.

When the invitation arrived several weeks ago, Jake had sent back the RSVP indicating he would be bringing a guest. At the time he'd thought he might ask one of the women he'd dated occasionally in the past. But that was before he'd fallen in love with Marcie. Now there was only one woman he wanted to have on his arm when he entered that room. No one would question why she was there, either. He'd make sure that everyone understood that she was his date, not his employee. It was a fantasy that brought a smile to his face.

That smile quickly disappeared, however, when he learned that he was needed in New York immediately. He would be gone three days—the last few days that Marcie would be in the office.

The remainder of the morning passed in a flurry as the usual demands of his office kept him occupied. Just before lunch, Sandra O'Neill phoned.

"I've found someone for you," she reported cheerfully.

"That was quick."

"Yes, well, I can't promise she'll be as efficient as Marcie, but she should do a good job. Speaking of Marcie, if you could fill out the evaluation form on her performance and send it over before you leave, I'd appreciate it."

"No problem."

After hanging up the phone, he sifted through the assortment of papers littering his desk until he found the lemon-yellow assessment record Sandra had sent over with the contract for temporary help. He had just finished giving Marcie high marks when she knocked on his door.

"These are urgent," she told him, entering the room. She handed him several legal documents.

He gave them a quick look, then told her about his trip to New York, instructing her as to what needed to be done in his absence.

"What day will you be returning?" she asked.

"I hope to be back on Friday evening, but I may have to stay over until Saturday morning. You haven't forgotten that we have a date, have you?"

"It's still on?"

She was standing beside his desk, and on an impulse, he pulled her down onto his lap.

"Jake! Someone might walk in!" she fretted.

He smiled wickedly. "I can't help myself." He loved having her in his arms. She was soft and warm and fitted perfectly. "Of course we're still on for Saturday. I want to show you off to all my friends. It's going to be a very special night."

He gave her a quick kiss and set her back on her feet.

"About Saturday night..." she began, smoothing the front of her skirt.

"What about it?"

"Would you mind if I met you at the hotel? I have several errands to run on Saturday and it would be much easier for me if I were to meet up with you downtown rather than have you come to pick me up."

He reached for her hand, unable to resist touching her. "I prefer to give my dates an escort from door to door, but if it's less of a rush for you, then I suppose I can make an exception."

"It will be easier." This time she bent and kissed him. "Thank you for being understanding. Should we meet in the hotel lobby?"

They agreed upon a time and then before he let her go he warned her, "There's no way I am *not* taking you home. Understand?"

She nodded and gave her hand a gentle tug to pull it away from his. "You'd better let me get back to work or else you're going to miss your plane this afternoon."

As she started to leave, he stopped her. "Wait." She turned and faced him, looking at him with an innocence that reminded him why she was so unlike any of the women he used to date.

"What do you need?" she automatically asked.

"Nothing." He rose to his feet and walked over to her. "Since I won't be here on your last day, I want to tell you that you've done an excellent job, Marcie. Sandra was right. You are the best."

She smiled. "Why, thank you, sir. I only did my job."

"It will be rewarded," he promised with a provocative grin. "You'll see how much I appreciate you on Saturday night."

"I'll look forward to that. Now, is there anything else I can do for you before you leave?"

"Tell Alicia I need to see her, please," he instructed. "Oh—and one other thing. Take Friday afternoon off. With pay. You've earned it."

Just as she was leaving, Alicia knocked on his door. Marcie went out as Alicia stepped in, both women exchanging greetings in the process.

As soon as the door had closed, Alicia asked, "Have you looked over those tax forms I sent you this morning?"

"Yes." He reached for a stack of papers on his desk. "Go ahead and process these," he said, handing them to her.

What he didn't realize was that mixed in with the papers was a Temporarily Yours employee evaluation form. It wasn't until he passed Alicia's desk on his way out of the office that he learned of the mistake.

She waved the lemon-yellow slip of paper in the air. "Jake, this was in with the tax forms—it's an evaluation form for Temporarily Yours."

"I wanted that to go out in today's mail. Would you see that it gets done?"

"Sure. Is this supposed to be for Marcie MacLean?"

"Yes." He frowned. "I thought I had written her name on it."

He was about to take the paper from her when she said, "It's not a big deal. I can fill in her name."

A glance at the clock told him he was running behind schedule. He thanked her and hurried toward the elevator, forgetting that he had filled out a similar form for the temp who had preceded Marcie—an evaluation he had never mailed.

The final days of Marcie's temporary assignment flew by. She had settled nicely into the routine of being Jake's assistant and had discovered that even if she hadn't fallen in love with him, she would have thought he was a good boss.

But she had fallen in love with him. She hadn't expected it to happen, but now that it had she was glad she'd refused to throw in the towel that first day when he tried to send her back to Temporarily Yours. She liked the challenges the job at the investment firm presented and she liked Jake.

As she cleared out her desk on Friday afternoon, she left several notes for Brenda, including one that had her phone number on it just in case Brenda needed to contact her. Then she took one last look in Jake's office and headed for Temporarily Yours to find out from Sandra where her next assignment would be.

"Am I glad to see you!" Sandra said when she walked into her office.

Marcie smiled. "It's nice to be wanted."

"Sit," she said, motioning for her to take a seat. "You're in such demand…if only the rest of my staff was so popular."

"I do my best," Marcie said, sitting down across from her. "So, where do I go next?"

"Ah, let's see," Sandra said, flipping through a small stack of papers on her desk. "I have a CPA looking for someone familiar with spreadsheets."

"That's me," Marcie said cheerfully.

"Unfortunately, it doesn't pay as well as the assignment you just completed,'' Sandra said, looking over the rim of her glasses.

Marcie sighed. ''I guess all good things must come to an end.''

Sandra removed her glasses and leaned forward, her elbows on her desk. ''Do you want to talk about it?''

Marcie frowned. ''Talk about what, Sandra?''

For the first time since Marcie had known her, the head of the agency looked uncomfortable, fidgeting with pencils and papers on her desk.

''Something's wrong, isn't it?'' Marcie now was the one shifting uneasily in her chair.

A seriousness had replaced Sandra's usual cheery demeanor. ''Did you have a problem getting along with Jake Campbell?''

''I was late a couple of times, but when I explained to Jake—er, Mr. Campbell—that it was because of Emma, he understood. Overall, he seemed very pleased with my work,'' she answered honestly.

''But you were late on several occasions?''

''Yes, but I made the time up so I wouldn't get docked,'' she quickly added. Seeing that something was definitely troubling her boss, she asked, ''Did he say something about my work?''

''Not to me personally…''

''But?'' When Sandra didn't add anything, Marcie said, ''Sandra, something's bothering you. What is it?''

She opened a desk drawer and pulled out a lemon-yellow sheet of paper. ''I received this today.'' She passed it to Marcie.

Marcie knew what it was without asking. It was an evaluation form. Every employer completed one when the temp's assignment was finished. She had seen dozens of them, all of them praising her work.

Curious, she glanced at the rating sheet. This one was not complimentary. Quite the contrary. Several words stood out, including "incompetent". Marcie's heart caught in her throat. But it was Jake's signature at the bottom that had her clutching her stomach.

"I don't understand. He was satisfied with my work. He told me so himself."

"Then you don't know why he would have written such an evaluation?"

"No." She felt close to tears. "You know what kind of an employee I am. I've been here for years and I've never had an evaluation like this. This has to be a mistake!"

"Your name is on the top and his signature is on the bottom," Sandra said quietly.

Marcie looked at the form and saw both her name and Jake's signature. It was like déjà vu. He had done the same thing he had done five years ago—given her a poor evaluation. What was worse was that this time he hadn't only interfered with her professional life, but her personal one, as well.

All the kisses and the talk about wanting to be more than a boss to her. He had led her to believe that she was the kind of woman he wanted in his personal life. Made her promises, given her hope...only to turn in a highly critical report on her.

And she didn't have a clue as to why.

"I should have realized that something wasn't right when he said he didn't want you for the next four weeks," Sandra commented.

Marcie's brow creased. "But he doesn't need me next week. His regular assistant is coming back on Monday."

"Oh—then he didn't tell you." This time there was a look of pity on Sandra's face.

"Tell me what?"

"His assistant resigned. Jake called me earlier this week to ask if I could find another temp until they could hire someone to permanently take the position."

"What?" Marcie could hardly believe her ears. "Are you sure?" It was a stupid question. Of course Sandra was sure. She hadn't made a success of Temporarily Yours by getting her signals crossed.

For Marcie's benefit, she held up another sheet of paper. "I have his request right here."

Suddenly, Marcie realized what it all meant. "He didn't want me to stay on any longer, did he?" She swallowed with difficulty, trying not to show how badly the news affected her.

"I'm sorry, Marcie. He specifically asked that the temp not be you," Sandra said sympathetically. "But don't you worry. I won't have any trouble finding you another spot."

Marcie wasn't worried about getting another position. What was creating such emotional havoc inside her was the fact that Jake didn't want her in the office. He had led her to believe that he thought she had done a wonderful job in Brenda's absence, told her how important she had become in his life, invited her to a dinner with his friends...only to turn around and fire her.

"I...I..." she stammered, not knowing what to say. Finally, she choked out, "I did a good job, Sandra. I know I did."

"And I don't doubt that for one minute. I understand that sometimes personalities clash...."

Marcie almost laughed out loud. Clashed? She wondered what Sandra would say if she knew what had really happened. That Jake had dated her...given her reason to believe that he was falling in love with her...promised her that he wasn't going to lose her now that he had found her.

Sadly, she realized that it hadn't been true. None of it. Lip service. That's all it had been. Not only was Marcie hurt, but she was angry. Why hadn't he at least told her about Brenda's resignation? *Because then he would have had to explain why he wasn't going to allow her to stay on*, a little voice answered inside her head.

"At least while you were there you earned good money," Sandra said in a practical tone.

"I won't get that kind of pay anywhere else," Marcie noted soberly.

"Unfortunately, no," Sandra agreed. "Unless you want to work nights."

"You mean three to eleven?"

"Actually, I was thinking about eleven to seven. The graveyard shift."

"You have assignments for that time period?"

"Yes." She slipped her glasses back in place and flipped through the Rolodex until she found the card she wanted. "It's a bank downtown...requires an accounting background, which you have. The position is for three months. Apparently, someone is going on maternity leave." She quoted the hourly figure plus the added night bonus.

Marcie mentally calculated what she could earn. "It would be more than I usually make," she said thoughtfully.

"But you would have to take the bus at night,"

Sandra pointed out. "If you could borrow someone's car, there's underground parking with security."

A car was a luxury she couldn't afford. Not yet. She was still paying off the hospital bill from the time Emma had needed to have surgery. Anger rose in her once more. Four more weeks in Jake's office would have meant she'd have the money to finally put paid to that hospital debt. But with one phone call and an evaluation form he had taken that opportunity away from her.

"I hate to see you work that shift, Marcie." Sandra's voice became rather maternal. "I was going to put you at an insurance company on your side of town. It's true the wages aren't as good, but it would be a day job."

Marcie chewed on her lip thoughtfully. "I'd rather have the money, Sandra. Can I think about this and let you know? I'd like to check with Peggy and make sure it's not going to be a problem."

"Of course. Call me after you've made a decision."

It wasn't the job at the bank that was on Marcie's mind the rest of the afternoon. It was Jake. She felt betrayed. As if all the hard work she had done had been for nothing. As if her feelings for him had been used and tossed away.

All the compliments he had given her on her performance in Brenda's absence, all the sweet things he had said to her about wanting her to be his girlfriend…had they all been lies? She thought he cared about her, that he understood how important it was for her to have a job that paid well. Yet he had sent in a bad work report on her and told Sandra he didn't want her working for him anymore.

She tried not to think about him at all. She had an

afternoon off, which meant she could tackle one of the many projects that still needed to be done in the apartment. Instead, she sat on the sofa, teary-eyed.

That was where she was when Peggy arrived home with Emma. Tim was with them. Marcie swiped at her eyes with the backs of her hands, not wanting them to see that she had been crying. She was successful in keeping Emma from seeing how upset she was, but she knew that Peggy and Tim were aware that something was wrong.

As soon as Tim offered to take Emma into the kitchen for a snack, Peggy confronted her sister. "All right, what's wrong?"

"I've lost my job."

"Sandra adores you. How could you lose your job?" Peggy demanded.

"Not at the temp agency." She went on to explain how Jake had not only requested a different temp for the next four weeks but had turned in a bad work report on her.

"This doesn't make any sense," Peggy said, reaching for her sister's hands. "Didn't you tell me you're going out with him tomorrow night to some fancy dinner?"

She nodded miserably. "*Was* going. I wouldn't cross the street with that guy now."

"Why would he ask you out to dinner if he felt that way about you?"

It was something Marcie couldn't figure out herself. "Maybe he thought the evaluation wouldn't get there until next week."

"That doesn't sound like the Jake you've talked about."

"Well, it is." She reached for a tissue and blew her

nose. "I should have known better. I knew what he was like when I worked for him before. He's cold and unfeeling and he uses people," she spat out bitterly.

Peggy put her arm around her, trying to console her. "Sandra knows your work history. She's not going to believe what he says."

"I can't believe he could be so nasty! You know how hard I worked…how many long hours I put in."

"Shh. Don't cry, Marcie. He's not worth it. He's just some jerk of a guy."

Marcie stiffened. "I'm not crying over him. I'm crying because of the injustice of it all." Again she had to blow her nose. "If I had been able to stay on with his company for another four weeks, I would have had enough money to pay off the hospital bills."

"You don't need to worry about Emma's medical bills," Peggy reassured her. "Tim told me he'd help out if I needed it."

The tears had finally stopped. Marcie looked at her sister and gave her a weak smile. "He said he'd do that?" Seeing her sister's nod, she said, "He's a good guy, Peggy. Hang on to him."

"I plan to," she said with a grin. "Now you have to put all of this behind you. I know you hate having anything bad on your record, but I doubt it's going to change your situation at Temporarily Yours. You're still Sandra's best employee and I bet she has dozens of jobs you can handle."

Marcie nodded. "You're right. She already has one lined up for me. I just wanted to check with you first. It's on the night shift."

They discussed the pros and cons of the bank position, with Marcie coming to the conclusion that it might be just the kind of change she needed. It would also help to alleviate any day-care problems Peggy might encounter.

"So now that you've made that decision, what are you going to do about tomorrow night?" Peggy wanted to know. "Maybe you should call Jake and give him a chance to explain. I mean, there could be a logical explanation for everything that's happened."

The suggestion earned her a stern look from her sister. "There is no excuse for what he did. I'm not going to give him another opportunity to use me. He led me to believe that..." she began, then thought better of it. Why tell her sister that she had foolishly fallen in love with Jake Campbell?

She stood. "It's in the past. I won't give him another chance to jeopardize my career. He's history. And if you and Tim want to go out tomorrow night, I'd be happy to sit with Emma. As far as Jake Campbell is concerned, he can rot for all I care."

CHAPTER TEN

ON SATURDAY evening Jake stood in the lobby of the Saint Paul Hotel, waiting for Marcie. He scrutinized the occupants of every taxi that stopped in front of the main entrance, wondering if she could have possibly misunderstood the time or the place they had agreed to meet.

He had told her seven, yet it was nearly half past and there was still no sign of her. He wondered if there was a problem at home. Maybe Emma was sick.

He pulled his mobile phone from his pocket and dialed her number. He received the answering machine—just as he had every other time he tried calling her that day.

And he had tried calling. At least a dozen times. Ever since his plane had landed at the airport he had wanted to hear her voice. That's why he became more agitated as time passed and she didn't arrive.

When another member of the dinner party came to the lobby to see what was keeping him, he knew he had no choice but to abandon his watch at the door and join the others. Leaving a message at the front desk and with the concierge, he reluctantly walked into the private dining room—not with Marcie on his arm as he'd planned, but alone.

"I thought you were bringing a guest," one of his colleagues remarked as he took his seat at the dinner table.

"I'm afraid she's been detained," he hedged, trying not to sound as perturbed as he was feeling.

"Should we wait a few minutes longer before ordering?"

"No, it's all right. I'm sure she'll be here shortly," he answered, although as the minutes continued to tick away, even he became skeptical. And concerned. He couldn't help but worry that she might have been involved in some kind of accident. It wasn't like her not to call and leave a message.

When the first course was served and there was still no sign of her, Jake excused himself to go make an inquiry at the front desk. To his relief, he was told there was a message for him. Eagerly, he listened as the clerk peered over a desktop littered with papers.

"You're Jake Campbell?" He confirmed her query with a nod. "Someone named Marcie called..." The woman paused, then said, "Oh."

"Oh what?" he asked.

She cleared her throat before saying, "She said to tell you you've been stood up. Sorry." She gave him an apologetic smile, but he didn't notice.

He was too stunned to notice anything. *Stood up?* "That's it? That's the entire message?" he demanded in a not so very nice tone of voice.

"I'm sorry, sir. That's all it says." She handed him the slip of paper upon which the hotel operator had scribbled the message.

He stared at the small scrap of paper in disbelief, then anger overwhelmed him. He crushed the message in his fist and stormed away from the desk.

Stood up? What was this? Marcie's idea of a bad joke? No, she was not one to play jokes. Then why was she behaving this way? Unless... He shook his head to rid himself of the idea. But it was no use. The more he thought about it, the more certain he was that there was only one other explanation for her behavior. She was getting revenge for his having fired her five years ago.

All the way back to the dining room, he fumed. How could he have been so stupid? Five years ago she had all but flaunted her unreliability in his face, and yet all she had had to do was bat those beautiful blue eyes at him and, like a lovesick schoolboy, he had played right into her hands. He felt like a first-class fool.

By the time he sat back down at the dinner table the second course had already been served. He tried to put on a cheerful face for the sake of the guests of honor. It wasn't easy. When he announced that his date wasn't going to be able to make it after all, he knew by the sympathetic looks he received that most of them suspected he had been stood up. He could have concocted an excuse for her, but he wasn't the kind of man to lie to cover up for anyone, not even himself.

So he quietly ate his dinner, knowing that everyone in the room suspected that his date had simply decided not to come. It was the ultimate humiliation for a man in his position. All his life he had prided himself on being a good judge of character, yet he had walked right into Marcie's web of revenge.

His laugh was self-deprecating. Only a few days ago he had bragged to several of his colleagues that he was bringing the girl of his dreams to the party. Now here he sat—alone—and the object of everyone's pity, thanks to Marcie.

When the party ended, he was tempted to drive over to her place and tell her in no uncertain terms what he thought of her. But he knew that she didn't live alone.

Her young niece would be sleeping in the apartment. If he went over there at midnight, he would create the kind of scene no mother would want her child to wake up to and witness.

So instead of doing what came naturally—finishing what he started—he went home and went to bed. It was a long time, however, before he was able to fall asleep.

Marcie had never stood up a guy in her entire life—until Jake, that is. Maybe that's why she carried the burden of guilt as if it were a ball and chain. It wasn't in her nature to run away from a confrontation, yet that's exactly what she had done. Instead of calling Jake and telling him how hurt she was by his evaluation, she chose to ignore him.

"He deserved it," she mumbled to herself as she fixed an egg salad sandwich.

"Who deserved what?" her sister asked as she came into the kitchen. "Or do I even need to ask? You're talking about Jake, aren't you?"

Marcie finished wrapping her sandwich. "I'd appreciate your not mentioning his name in my presence. As far as I'm concerned, he doesn't exist."

"Ha!"

"He doesn't!" she insisted, adding an apple and a carton of yogurt to her brown bag.

Peggy let the subject slide and said, "I hate to see you going to work in the middle of the night."

"Yes, well, I wouldn't have to if you know who had simply let me continue doing the splendid job I was doing for him," she said irritably. "And I was doing a good job—no, I was doing an *excellent* job."

As she shoved a drawer shut with more force than

was necessary, Peggy said, "I still think there's got to be an explanation for what he did."

"Yeah. He's a rat." She gave her sister a stern look.

Peggy wisely changed the subject. "Why don't you let Tim at least give you a ride to work? You can take the bus home in the morning, but we both would feel better if he drove you."

"I can get there on my own," she said stubbornly.

"I know you can, but Tim is going to come over and take you anyway." As Marcie finished tidying up the kitchen, Peggy said, "For Pete's sake, Marcie, if you don't quit slamming things, you're going to wake up Emma."

Marcie's shoulders sagged. "I'm pathetic, aren't I?"

"No, you're reacting like a person who's been hurt." Peggy slung an arm around her shoulder and gave a squeeze of sympathy.

"I've had to struggle so hard for money..." Marcie began, then heaved a long sigh.

"This isn't about money, sis. It's about Jake. The reason you're so upset is because you feel betrayed by him."

To Marcie's dismay, tears welled in her eyes. "He told me he wanted to take me to that fancy dinner so he could show all his friends that he'd finally found a woman who was special." Peggy opened her arms and Marcie went into them, seeking the same comfort she had so often given her sister in the past.

"He must care about you, Marcie. He's called enough times," she pointed out.

"He probably wanted to chew me out for not showing up at the party," she said on a sniffle.

"Maybe he misses you," Peggy suggested gently.

Marcie hiccuped as she pushed herself away from

her sister. "H-how can you say that? You know what he did." She swiped at the tears with the backs of her hands. "Look, I don't want to talk about him. I've learned my lesson. I was just a diversion for him, that's all."

Peggy didn't try to console her. Just then the doorbell rang, startling Marcie. "Don't worry. It's only Tim. I told you he was going to take you to work."

Marcie gave her a grateful smile. "Do me a favor, will you?"

"Sure, what is it?"

"If Jake calls again, please don't give him any information about me."

Peggy looked as if she wanted to argue the point but reluctantly agreed before going to answer the door.

Marcie knew the day was going to come when she would be able to tell Jake Campbell in a dispassionate voice exactly what she thought of him as a boss and as a man. Right now, the hurt was too painful, but someday she would be strong enough to face him. And when she did...well, she'd make him regret the day he ever decided to send that bad work report to Sandra.

It had been one week since Jake had seen or heard from Marcie. One long, agonizing week in which he'd gradually let go of some of the anger he felt toward her. The replacement Sandra O'Neill had sent over from Temporarily Yours had proved to be well trained and capable of doing the job, but she lacked something— he didn't know what.

That wasn't true. He did know what separated the efficient Gloria from the efficient Marcie. Intuition. For some reason unknown to him, Marcie could anticipate his every whim. The longer they worked together, the

better she became at knowing just what it was he
needed. If he didn't know better, he would have
thought she could read his mind.

Despite how Marcie had humiliated him, he had
been softening toward her all week long. Instead of
wanting to call her and read the riot act, he found himself wondering whether she regretted giving him the
brush-off the way she had. He needed to focus on business, which is why he was relieved when Gloria buzzed
him with the news he had a call on line one.

But long after the phone call had ended, Marcie was
still in Jake's thoughts. In fact, she was on his mind
more than he wanted to admit. It didn't help that when
he went home at night Clara asked about her. Or that
at least half a dozen times during the day someone in
the office mentioned her name.

Although he was not an impulsive man, Jake did
something he hadn't planned to do on his way to work
one morning. He drove to Marcie's apartment. As he
parked the Porsche across the street from her building,
he saw a taxi pull over to the curb. Inside was a woman
with blond, springy curls. As she climbed out, Jake saw
that it was Marcie.

She paid the driver, then hurried up the steps before
pausing to dig for her keys in her purse. Then she
opened the front door and slipped inside.

Jake could only stare in disbelief. She was just coming home, which meant she had been gone all night.
Where had she been...and with whom? They were
questions that troubled him. He thought about all the
times he had called the apartment only to have Peggy
tell him she wasn't home. He thought she'd been lying,
but now he wasn't so sure.

"You shouldn't call here anymore," Peggy had told

him on more than one occasion. He didn't realize the significance of those words until now. Peggy knew what he hadn't wanted to admit. Marcie wasn't interested in him. She never had been and now it was apparent that she spent her nights away from home.

Jake started the car's engine and drove away from the curb, his tires squealing as he pulled out into traffic. He tried not to think what a fool he had been.

Normally, Jake ate his lunch in the office unless he had business to conduct over the noon meal. However, when his grandmother had announced she wanted to have lunch with her favorite grandson, he couldn't say no.

The place she picked was a small outdoor café near the university. Although the air was still a bit cool, patrons flocked to the restaurant, enjoying the opportunity to dine outside.

As usual, Jake found his grandmother's company soothing. She had a way about her that reminded him that life could have a slower pace. She also appreciated the little things—like the scent of lilacs that wafted across the patio. Every time she mentioned how much she loved their fragrance, he smiled fondly.

As they were leaving the restaurant, she announced she needed to use the ladies' room. Jake told her he'd wait for her near the entrance.

It was while he stood outside the front door that he encountered Marcie's sister, Peggy. Coming up the walk, she wore the same uniform as the other staff who worked in the café.

"Mr. Campbell!" She looked as surprised to see him as he was to see her.

"Ms. MacLean. You work here?"

"Yes. If you'll excuse me." If looks could chill a person, he figured he'd be an ice cube by now.

"Give my regards to Marcie," he said as she reached for the door handle.

That had her turning back around to face him. "And why should I do that?" Her voice was hostile, as were her eyes. "After everything that's happened, I'd say that's a rather offensive comment to make to me, her sister."

"You'll have to forgive me, Ms. MacLean, but I fail to see why I should be the object of her disdain," he said stiffly. "I'm the one who got stood up...or did your sister fail to mention that?"

Her mouth dropped open and she stared at him, speechless. Then she slowly shook her head, saying, "You're something else, you know that?"

"Me?" This time, he was the one with disbelief on his face.

"Did you honestly think she'd want to go out with you after you gave her that bad work report?" She shook her head, then pulled open the door. "My sister worked darn hard for you. Then you do something like that. You ought to be ashamed of yourself." And with those words she disappeared inside the restaurant.

Just as she went in, his grandmother came out. She took his arm, patting it lovingly. "You're such a sweet boy. Thank you for the lunch. It was so peaceful, wasn't it?"

Jake almost laughed at the irony. Nothing about his conversation with Marcie's sister had been peaceful. As he walked his grandmother back to the car, he realized that it was probably a good thing he had run into Peggy MacLean. At least now his suspicions had been confirmed.

The reason Marcie had stood him up was because she had wanted to get revenge for something that had happened five years ago. It was a sobering thought. The feelings she had professed to have for him had all been part of her plan to get even.

Maybe now that he had learned the truth he could finally put her out of his thoughts.

As hard as Jake tried, he still couldn't stop thinking about Marcie. His conversation with Peggy had left him disgruntled and crabby. It was no secret around the firm that he was in a bad mood and he had even overheard someone say that he was on a reign of terror. It was a conversation with Sandra O'Neill that changed everything.

"Jake," her cool voice came over the wire, "I don't know what you're doing over there, but my temp is threatening to refuse to come to your office if you don't lighten up a bit."

Jake rubbed the bridge of his nose and sighed. "Sorry, Sandra. What if I promise not to eat any more temps? Will that help?"

"No. You've lost your credibility. What's wrong with you anyway?"

"I don't know," he said. "I've got some personal problems and I suppose they're seeping into my work."

"Seeping? You mean flooding, don't you? Even I have noticed you're not your usual self."

"What do you mean?" Jake didn't want to have this conversation. Sandra was an astute business person and having her call him on the carpet only added insult to injury.

"You've forgotten Marcie's evaluation? Jake, come on. I wouldn't do that to my worst enemy!"

"What are you talking about? I gave her a glowing review."

He heard a sardonic chuckle. "If that's glowing, I'd hate to see an unfavorable one. You were brutal. If I didn't know how good Marcie is, I would have fired her on the spot."

"Sandra, what are you talking about? I gave her an excellent review. Aren't you listening to me?"

"I'm listening, but I also know what's in front of my own eyes. Jake, I can't say I'm eager to send over any of the temps if you're going to be so nasty to them."

"I wasn't nasty to Marcie!" he exclaimed.

"Well, someone was. I'll fax you a copy of the evaluation so you can see for yourself."

Jake started as the phone clicked. She'd hung up on him. In a moment, his fax line buzzed and a single page of paper scrolled out of the machine.

It was an evaluation form with Marcie's name on the top and his signature at the bottom. Every negative that could be assigned to her performance had been checked along with several disparaging comments. He stared at it in disbelief.

Sandra was right. He had filled out the form—not for Marcie—for her predecessor. He felt a sinking feeling in his gut. He rummaged through several papers on his desk until he came to the evaluation form he *thought* he had forwarded to Sandra.

"Oh, no." Jake dropped his head into his hand and closed his eyes. No wonder Marcie was angry. She'd no doubt read the form complaining of her poor work habits, ethics and even slovenly dress—an evaluation that had absolutely nothing to do with her!

With a determination that he'd rarely felt in his lifetime, Jake punched the number for Alicia and demanded that she come to his office immediately.

"Yes, sir?" Alicia came into the office looking worried.

Jake felt a little guilty. He had been a real bear this week and obviously Alicia thought she was next in line for a mauling.

"Do you remember the evaluation you asked me about a couple of weeks ago—the one I told you to send to Sandra O'Neill?"

Alicia looked puzzled for a moment before a light of recognition dawned on her face. "Do you mean Marcie's evaluation?"

Jake's gut tightened. "Did you mail it?"

"Yes, don't you remember? You had forgotten to put her name on, so I added it even though it didn't make any sense to me. I mean, everyone in the office thinks Marcie is great and the evaluation...well, it wasn't very complimentary."

"That's because you had the wrong form." His head was beginning to throb.

"Sir?"

"It was for the temp before Marcie."

"Oh, so that's why it was so negative." Then a horrified look spread across Alicia's features. "But I sent it to Ms. O'Neill as Marcie's!"

"Bingo."

"Oh my gosh! Marcie must feel awful!"

"Right again."

"I'll call her and tell her what I did. I had no idea—"

"It's not your fault, Alicia, it's mine. I was in too much of a hurry to check that form before I asked you to send it. You were only doing your job."

"I should have asked you about it," she said with regret. "I should have known you wouldn't have given her a bad work report." A look of horror crossed her face. "She didn't lose her job at the temp agency, did she?"

"No, but I need to clear this up with Sandra O'Neill," he told her, dismissing her with an assurance that all would be well.

Alicia backed out the door apologizing, but Jake simply waved her away. He didn't know how he was going to get Marcie to listen to him, but one way or another he would.

No one answered the MacLeans' phone. No matter what time of day he called, Jake got no answer. His patience at an end, he went to her apartment and pounded on the door. Even if he had to wake little Emma, he was going to speak to Marcie.

As he stood there banging his fist against the wood, an elderly woman from across the hall stuck out her head and scowled at him from beneath the pink sponge rollers she wore in her hair. She watched him slam his fist against the door. "You're wasting your time."

"They're not home?"

The woman sniffed as if she was insulted not to have been asked sooner. "They're running around half the night, those people. I don't know what's going on, but it probably ain't good. Sometimes the one comes draggin' in at dawn. I don't know what's come over young people these days. Why, when I was young—"

"Thank you." Jake turned and left while she reminisced.

Back in his car, he drummed his fingertips on the steering wheel and frowned. Marcie, running around "half the night"? That didn't sound like her. But then lately, he hadn't been sure he knew just who the real Marcie was.

Or where she was, he realized as time passed and there was still no sign of her. There was only one thing he was sure of—he was going to talk to her no matter what. Even if it meant spending the night in his car waiting for her to return.

Which is exactly what happened. He dozed off, waking only when the sound of a door slamming broke the silence. Jake sat up so quickly he rammed his rib cage into the steering wheel. Still gritting his teeth in pain, he watched Marcie get out of a car, give the male driver a sweet smile, then turn and go into her building.

Out all night. Another man. Jake counted to ten to calm himself. Now what? Had Marcie jumped out of the frying pan and into the fire? Or, more aptly, out of one disappointing relationship into an even more meaningless one?

He sat there a while longer trying to bring his anger—at both himself and at Marcie—under control. He didn't even see Peggy bearing Emma on one hip walk up to his car.

When she tapped on the window, he rolled it down.

"What on earth are you doing out here?" Peggy asked. "Are you spying on my sister after breaking her heart?"

Jake started to protest but stopped when he realized that that was exactly what he was doing. "I wanted to apologize to her and no one was home last night,'' he told her.

"Of course there was no one home. Because of you, my sister's had to work the night shift at the bank."

"She was at work last night?"

"Yes, as if it's any business of yours. She's been there ever since you refused to let her stay on. She made me promise to take Emma to Tim's on the nights she was gone so we wouldn't be alone. That's how Marcie is—always worrying about others."

"But what about the other man?"

"What other man?"

"The one who dropped her off here this morning."

Peggy shrugged. "Probably someone from the bank who gave her a ride home so she wouldn't have to take the bus. I could ask her..." Her face softened and a slow grin spread across her features. "Are you jealous?"

There was no use denying it now. He'd made a royal fool of himself too many times to attempt to redeem himself now. "I didn't mean to hurt her, Peggy. There was a terrible mix-up at the office and her name was put on an evaluation meant for another employee."

"You mean you didn't say all those terrible things about my sister's work performance?"

"Absolutely not. She's the finest assistant I've ever had. I don't ever want to let her go again."

"You mean you'll hire her back?" Peggy looked excited.

"No. She's not going to work for me. I have other plans for the two of us."

Peggy gave a squeak of delight and opened the car door. "Well, then come on in. You've got to tell this to Marcie."

Marcie was sitting at the kitchen table when her sister burst into the room, dragging Jake behind her. Stunned, she glared at him and asked, "What are you doing here?"

"He's come to tell you something," Peggy answered for him. "So if you two will excuse me and Emma—"

"No—Peggy, don't go!" Marcie begged. The last thing she wanted was to be alone in a room with the man who had been so cruel to her. She needed all the support she could get, including Peggy's.

"Sorry, Marcie, but you need to talk to Jake alone," Peggy said with a wink and carried Emma out of the room.

"What did you tell her?" Marcie said in an accusing tone of voice.

"That I needed to talk to you."

"Why? You said everything you needed to say on that evaluation form you sent Sandra O'Neill."

To Marcie's amazement, he dropped to one knee, took her limp fingers in his own. "I owe you an apology, Marcie. Because of my carelessness, a bad work report was turned in with your name on it. When you're not there, my office doesn't operate as efficiently and the result was that an evaluation for a previous temp accidentally made its way to Sandra's office."

He stood up and pulled another yellow evaluation form from his pocket and handed it to her. "This is the form that should have been sent to Sandra O'Neill."

Marcie read it and her eyes misted. "You really mean all these nice things you've written?"

"Of course." He went on to explain how the mix-up had occurred, conveying Alicia's apologies, as well.

"But when you learned Brenda had quit, why did you tell Sandra you didn't want me to stay on?" Marcie asked, her heart still aching at the memory.

"Because if you were my employee, I couldn't let the world know that I love you, could I? There is a rule at the firm about bosses having romances with their administrative assistants, you know," he told her with a grin that made her go weak at the knees.

She stared at him in disbelief, not quite sure she had heard correctly. "You love me?" she repeated.

"Yes, and I hope you're going to say that you love me, too." He gave her such an endearing look she couldn't help but fling her arms around his neck and hug him tight.

"Of course I love you," she said in delight, loving the feel of his arms around her.

He kissed her then, long and hard, erasing any doubts she may have had that this was a dream. When they finally drew apart, there was so much love in Jake's eyes that tears of happiness welled in Marcie's own.

He touched a gentle finger to her cheek. "You bring joy and excitement to my life, Marcie. I don't ever want to lose that. I don't ever want to lose you."

"Ever?" She held her breath, wondering if it meant what she hoped it did.

He kissed her again and pledged, "Never. It's been agony since you walked out of my life. No one in the office can replace you, but I can put up with the most inefficient of assistants if I know you'll be waiting for me when I come home at night."

"Does this mean what I think it means?"

He raised her fingertips to his lips and kissed them. "I want you to be my wife, Marcie."

Overcome emotionally, she couldn't speak. The tears that had been welling in her eyes spilled over onto her cheeks.

He swiped at them with the pads of his thumbs. "I hope these are 'yes' tears."

"They are."

"Good."

"It's just that I never expected this would happen when I saw you again," she said in amazement.

He grinned. "That makes two of us. I've discovered that things never work out quite as I plan when I'm around you…but I like it."

Happier than he'd ever been in his life, he kissed his bride-to-be.